The
SCOT'S
LEGACY

HIGHLAND HUNTERS ❀ 8

KEIRA
MONTCLAIR

CHAPTER ONE

Spring, 1316, the Highlands of Scotland

A LARIC GRANT GUIDED his horse down the treacherous incline, praying they'd make it to the bottom safely. Three Grant guards had made it down before him, and several others, including his father Jamie and brother Els, still waited their turn. Once down, Alaric turned to his father and waved.

"Ye can make it. The storm is nearly upon us, but ye have time. We have to get the seed in." His brother, Els, rode behind his father, the large bags of seed they'd just purchased settled across each horse. The seed was worth every bit of gold they'd paid for it, after last year's famine. But if it got wet, it would be ruined.

When his father and brother were halfway down the slope, big fat drops of rain splattered around them, wetting the ground too quickly.

"Hurry! Ye can make it."

The others in their group waited at the top to see if the two made it safely before attempting their own descent.

As Alaric watched, the horses' hooves slid on the wet, hard-packed clay. He bellowed to the others behind his brother, "Go around!"

He wasn't sure they heard, because just then, the skies opened, rain falling in sheets, slanting across the landscape, and the incline became a river. In moments, the terrifying sound of a horse losing its footing rang out, and the scene in front of him moved in slow motion. Everything in Alaric Grant's life changed in an instant.

His father's horse careened down the slope, front hooves catching on a stone as they slid, sending both rider and mount catapulting to the bottom of the rocky hill. The chieftain of Clan Grant bellowed in pain with every impact. His horse landed well away from him, one small favor that may have saved his life.

They'd been off to a neighboring clan to purchase seeds for their spring planting, patrolling along the way. When they noticed the storm on the horizon, they tried to rush to save the seed, Alaric suggesting they take the incline back to the keep. It was risky in bad weather, but he'd made it down with his horse easily.

Why the hell hadn't they taken the long way around? The safe way?

Alaric dismounted to help his sire, and he cringed when he looked at him, knowing he'd broken at least one bone from the way his limbs were bent. At the sound of pebbles and small stones on the slope, he glanced up to see his older brother and his mount suffer the same fate as his sire. Els's horse also lost his footing on the hill, sending Els into the air. His brother landed hard on his head and rolled down the incline.

Alaric wished to hop back on his horse to race in the opposite direction, as far away as possible, but years of his father's and grandfather's and uncle's teachings made him do the right thing. He hurried to his father's side first, praying he was still alive. He'd tend to Els in a moment.

At the bottom of the embankment, he barked orders to the guards as the storm continued to batter them, drenching them with heavy rain. Snow would have been better, but the rain fell, freezing in some places on the ground, making the journey even more treacherous.

He shouted at the group of men still considering venturing down the hill. "Take the other path! Go that way." He motioned them to the longer but safer path. The entire group finally headed toward the longer option.

Alaric continued to give orders as the men arrived from the other path.

"Go to the keep for the carts. Take the seed with ye and keep it dry." He pointed to the large bags on the two horses.

"Tell my mother to ready the healing chamber for multiple injured."

"Check the two horses. See if they can stand."

Guards rushed to do his bidding. One raced off to the keep to fetch help while the others tended to the horses and the precious seed. The famine had made all the clans desperate to be sure their plantings would be successful this spring, and they were readying for the season in as many ways as possible.

Confident that his orders were being followed, Alaric turned back to his father. Jamie Grant lay in a heap, all mud from his fall.

"Da!" Alaric called out as he knelt next to him, afraid to touch him. Aunt Jennie had always said to check the injured before moving them. She's lectured everyone about how moving someone the wrong way could make an injury worse.

"Hand me the blanket on my horse," he yelled to one of the guards. "Da, can ye hear me?" He leaned over him to listen for breathing sounds before feeling for the beat of his life's blood pulsing through him.

His father opened his eyes and groaned, "My leg."

Alaric did a quick check of him, the oddly bent leg most concerning. He had blood on his trews and some on the ground around him, but nothing that looked heavy.

"Da, dinnae move. I have to check Els. Yer leg is broken, I've sent for a cart."

"I'm fine. Els fell too?"

Alaric could hear the sound of the cart wheels approaching. It must have been in a nearby field to have arrived this quickly.

One guard stood with the blanket. "Do ye wish for me to pick him up, Alaric? I can put him on yer horse."

"Nay!" Alaric didn't wish to yell, but had the fool no common sense? "His leg is broken. Cover him with the blanket while we wait for the cart.

It will surely take two of us to move him. Dinnae try to move him on yer own."

Uncle Connor arrived. He'd been riding toward the back of their company and must have just come in on the longer path. "What happened, Alaric?"

"Both mounts lost their footing. Da's leg is broken so dinnae move him yet. I have to check Els. And send the rest of the men back. This storm is getting worse and there is no need to keep more men than necessary, or there will be more injuries. The horses are all unsettled by Midnight Moon's fall."

Els hadn't moved, so Alaric knelt next to him and tapped his shoulder. "Els, wake up."

His cousin Alick joined him, riding in just behind Uncle Connor and leaping off his horse.

"He looks dead," he whispered to Alaric.

"He's breathing." Alaric reached for the blood pulsing in his neck. "Strong heart still. Do ye see any wounds? Any blood or broken bones?"

Alick sighed, feeling through the man's ripped trews. "Nay. I'll put him on my horse and take him back. Your sire needs the cart and there's only one."

"Wait," Alaric called out as Alick lifted Els with the help of another guard. "His head. I see something." He ran his hand over the back of his head. "He has a bump starting just there. Get him to the keep. I'll take care of Da."

Two guards helped get Els on the horse in front of Alick and then arranged him the best they could, protecting him from the rain.

"And take all the ones hanging about with ye," Alaric shouted after them. He noticed a number of guards nearby staring, wishing to see how badly the two were injured. "Leave two men to travel back with us."

He glanced at Uncle Connor who nodded and said, "I'll stay with ye, Alaric. He's my only brother. We have to move him carefully."

His sire opened his eyes, the pain evident. "I shouldn't have tried it, Connor. Midnight did not wish to go down but I pushed him."

Joya, Els's wife, burst into the space, panting and frantic. "Els!" she screamed.

"Get them both out of this weather, Alick," Alaric said. "Dinnae worry about us. Go."

"Come, Joya," Alick said softly. "Ye'll do him no good out here, catching your death." Joya nodded and clambered up behind one of the guards, and the bulk of the group headed toward the keep. The two injured horses were up and moving, thankfully. Both were still skittish but they were walking without much problem other than some cuts and scrapes from the rocks.

The two remaining guards moved the cart closer to Jamie.

His father hadn't fared so well, though he and Els had both bounced while the horses slid. "Move the cart over here."

"Alaric, tell yer mother I need her," his father said.

"I already sent word, Da. Uncle Connor is going to help me lift ye into the cart. We'll be careful as we can, but yer leg looks broken."

"And one arm too, I fear," his father mumbled. "Just get me to Gracie."

His parents still adored each other after all these years, and they were often teased affectionately about it. It gave Alaric hope that someday he'd find the same with the right lass, but he'd had no luck up to this point.

Alaric gave instructions to one guard. "Put the blanket underneath, Hugh. Get the one from yer horse, Uncle Connor. He'll need that to prop the leg. I'll cover him with mine. I have one dry one yet. Hugh, hold the cart still while we settle him. We cannae have it sliding in the mud."

Once the blanket was under Jamie, Connor and Alaric used it to move his father into the cart. His father only cursed them out once. "Hellfire, this isnae what I needed."

"Mama will fix ye, Da."

Connor added, "Ye'll have to slow down like she's been telling ye, Jamie. Ye just dinnae listen."

Connor and Jamie were the two chieftains of the clan since their brother Jake had passed on. Connor was younger than Jamie. Their three sisters, Kyla, Elizabeth, and Maeve, also helped keep the clan running efficiently and peacefully.

A horse approached as they eased the cart forward. It was his father's second and Kyla's husband, Finlay. "Hell, Jamie. Ye stay strong, Chief. What can I do, Alaric?"

"Ride along next to him and make him keep still. He cannae be moving that leg." Alaric had to admit he surprised himself with his instructions.

He was no healer, but apparently he'd been around his mother enough to learn something.

They headed back to the keep, moving slowly in the rain, but there were no other problems. The horses all made it back, the seed had been handled, and Els was already in the healing chamber by the time they arrived.

Alaric needed his brother to wake up and his father to heal. He had to pray both would be on the mend soon, because he planned to head out on patrol again. Maitland Menzie, one of the leads on the Scots' patrols, would be here shortly to gather a group of riders for the next one.

And he needed a distraction. This experience was too close to the one event in his past that he tried hardest to forget. Seeing his father and brother incapacitated so quickly brought that dreaded memory to the fore. The one day he wished he could forget because there was no fixing what had happened that day.

The worst day of his life.

CHAPTER TWO

ELISANT RAMSAY CAME into the Ramsay great hall from their family tower with the intent of going out to the archery field to practice, but she stopped as soon as she noticed the crowd gathered there. So many of her cousins sat about chatting that it reminded her of the Yule festivities.

She ventured over to the side table and grabbed a hunk of bread then took a seat near the hearth, waiting to hear what all the chatter was about. To her surprise, it appeared they were discussing their next patrol, which she'd been hoping would start soon.

"Eli, so glad ye joined us. Ye'll wish to hear this." Reyna waved at her. "The next patrol is leaving soon, and there arenae many going. Will ye join the patrol?"

"Of course. Tell me more." She took a bite of the crusty dark bread she loved, dipping it into a small bowl of honey on a table nearby.

Reyna flipped her long dark plait off her shoulder, then continued. "Grandda received word that the English are restless in Berwick

Castle. It seems they are nearly starving and Edward hasnae sent any rations for them. James Douglas has heard they will be leaving the safety of the castle to look for food."

Eli shrugged, not really understanding all that was going on with Edward, the king of England, and the Scottish king, Robert the Bruce. It seemed the two were always at odds with each other, and she never paid much attention to the specific incidents.

"That happened before. They headed to market at Edinburgh to steal. We caught many of them then. Is that no' right?"

"Aye, Dyna and Thea were there, but this is different," Isla offered, lifting her eyes from the garment she worked on. "Douglas has heard a large number have been sent out together in search of cattle. Ye ran into a few in Edinburgh."

Ysenda said, "They are intent on *stealing* cattle this time." She rubbed her leg, but Eli was glad to see her sister freely moving about after breaking it last winter in an avalanche. Though she hadn't expected her dear sister to fall for Lewis Haggert so quickly.

Sometimes it felt as though she'd lost her sister.

"So who is going on patrol?" She glanced from face to face, no one answering right away. After a long pause, she asked. "No one?"

Reyna said, "Isla and I are returning to Black Isle with our husbands. Perrin will go with us. We dinnae wish to travel when we are too far along, and we wish to be near our mamas when we have our bairns."

Ysenda snorted. "Ye know how I feel. I'll never go on patrol again after what happened to me in the avalanche. Lewis might go, but I think I've convinced him to wait until the next one. My leg isnae that strong yet. I'm still limping."

Eli couldn't argue that point. Besides, she knew how particular her mother was. If Ysenda went, Eli would have to stay home. Their mother wouldn't allow both daughters on the same patrol.

Tryana said, "I'm carrying too, so Cadyn will be staying back."

"That shrinks our numbers quite a bit," Eli said, rubbing her cheek absent-mindedly. She stopped the moment she realized what she was doing. She hated the habit—it gave away too much of her thinking.

"What's wrong?" Ysenda asked. "I know that look." Her sister knew what the cheek rub meant. Something was indeed bothering her.

Eli let out a whoosh of a sigh. "So that means on the patrol will be Dyna and Maitland. Me." She paused to go back to the original list of the patrol. Isla, Grif, Reyna, Wulf, Cadyn, Ysenda, Lewis, Thea... "Thea? Are she and Willum coming?"

"Nay," her grandfather Logan said, entering the hall from the outside, banging it with a wee bit more vigor than usual. "Donnan isnae completely healed yet, so she is staying with her mother. Willum has agreed to stay with her unless ye are desperate for him. He's promised to do Donnan's work on the raised crop beds they have, just in case we have another deluge of rain this season."

Most of Europe and England had gone through drenching rains last summer, causing famine due to the ruined crops. Donnan had worked out a way to keep his family's crops out of the soggy ground, so they'd been better off than most.

Her grandsire moved closer to Eli. "I know what ye are wondering, so I'll help where I can. Ceit is on Cameron land, I presume, and staying with Brin. I would expect nothing else. Patrolling isnae in her future now. Her failing eyesight unsettles her. And now that he is chieftain of Clan Cameron, Brin has too many responsibilities." Grandda paused for a moment before continuing, "So 'twill be Dyna, Maitland, ye, Wenna, Tevis, and Alaric."

She sighed again and rolled her eyes.

Isla grinned. "Who is it ye dinnae like, lass?"

"Alaric," her grandda announced.

"Grandda!" she shouted, perhaps a wee bit too loud.

The man arched his brow at her. "Ye should spend more time with him. 'Twould be a great alliance between the clans. Ceit did her duty with Clan Cameron. Someone needs to solidify the Grant alliance. And I wish ye'd do it before I die."

She opened her mouth to speak, but then closed it. She couldn't think of anyone else for Alaric. "Mayhap Alaric doesnae wish to marry."

Ysenda giggled. "I think ye should ask him. Ye two would make a cute couple."

"But I dinnae wish to marry Alaric." She nearly stomped her foot but stopped at the last moment.

"Then dinnae. Find someone else. Look who Reyna found on patrol. Ye could do the same."

That gave her the perfect opportunity to roll her eyes with as much emphasis as she could produce. This conversation was getting old.

"When are we leaving?" she asked her grandfather.

"In two days. Maitland will be here to gather the group. Yer mother accepts that ye will go with the group."

"I planned on going, Grandsire. I liked the last patrol, I just wish there were more going."

"Good because 'tis yer time. Yer country needs ye. All yer cousins stepped up when they were needed. 'Tis yer turn now."

She sighed again, not wishing to argue with the man because she knew what that would bring her. More lecturing, more practicing in the fields, and then the same from her parents, because her grandfather would tell her father about any transgression she committed.

Reyna said, "Go on patrol, Eli. Ye need to get out there and see the world beyond Clan Ramsay. Each patrol travels to a different area or city. Ye'll meet many Scots along the way. I'm glad I did."

Ysenda asked, "Or do ye have yer eye on someone else?"

"I'll be out in the stable with Torrian." Her grandfather looked at her and said, "Pack yer things." Then he left.

Isla waited for the Ramsay elder to leave, then whispered, "Who is it? Ye must have yer eye on someone. Is it Alaric?"

"Nay!" she shouted, bolting out of her seat. "No one. I'm going to the archery field."

She left, a burst of giggles following her.

Why were lasses so ridiculous sometimes? Men. Who said she needed a man? What could they do for her that she couldn't do herself?

The giggling infuriated her so much that she stuck her head back in the door. "I dinnae need a man. I am no' interested in any man in either clan or on patrol." There. That should put an end to it.

"Ye may no' need one, but once ye find out what they can do for ye, ye might wish ye had one." Reyna's voice carried to her, and as much as Eli wished to slam the door like her grandfather, her cousin had her curiosity going.

"Why?" She narrowed her gaze at Reyna, whose temperament had changed now that she was married to Wulfstan. She was always happy. Sometimes too happy. What the devil was she referring to?

All the conversation stopped as they all gazed at her. Then Reyna said, "Ye truly dinnae know?"

"I know enough. I've heard all yer giggles before, but why do ye love it so?" She thought it a fair question. Even the serving lasses talked about a man's member.

Reyna ran her tongue across her lips and said, "Because it's so hot."

"Why does that matter?"

"We need to have a talk with ye, Eli. I forget ye are inexperienced in some ways. We'll meet in yer chamber after the fire is out this eve."

"Never mind." She spun on her heel and closed the door behind her. Whenever her cousins talked like this, it was as if she were naught but a wee bairn and she hated it.

CHAPTER THREE

A LARIC GOT UP as soon as he opened his eyes the next morning, hopping out of bed and donning his trews and tunic. He rinsed his mouth with water, using the tooth cleaning cloth, ran his fingers through his wild hair, then headed down the stairs to the hall to check on his sire and brother.

Dyna sat at a trestle table while her three bairns ate their meal. There were a few others about, but the air was full of tension.

He understood why. Last eve, he'd checked on his sire and brother before he went to bed. Neither had been in good shape.

"Good morn to ye, Dyna. Any changes for either one?"

Dyna shook her head, her long, white-blonde plait moving with the swing of her head. "Aunt Jennie is on her way. They hope she'll be here by this eve. We need another healer and soon. Yer poor mother is exhausted."

He nodded. "I'll check with her. I can watch over them while she sleeps. Any word on patrol?" He was ready to go on the morrow. As soon as

Els woke up, he'd leave with no worries. *If* Els woke up.

"Maitland should be on his way. Probably arriving with Aunt Jennie. He was already heading this way. We're assigned to the Borderlands again, not far from Berwick. I'll explain later."

"Who will be joining us for this trip?" Their last group had been small, so he was hoping for a larger one this time. He preferred at least eight on patrol.

"Only six. The three of us plus Eli, Tevis, and Wenna."

He let out a low whistle. That was smaller than he'd hoped for. He instantly translated the information to the important pieces. Three archers, three swordsmen. Could be worse. There'd been only four once, and they'd remained unscathed.

He was pleased to hear Eli was joining them. He enjoyed their verbal sparring. It kept him alert. "What about Astra or Hagen? We could use more archers." Dyna's siblings had both been trained in archery.

"Ye cannae be serious about Astra. She prefers a sword to a bow, and they are both terrible on patrol. They cannae pay attention. Please dinnae mention them to my sire. He'd send them along, and they arenae safe in my opinion."

Alaric smiled, knowing how protective Dyna was of her two younger siblings. Still, her misgivings were serious concerns, so he let the idea drop. "'Tis a fine group. I'll go see my mother." He grabbed half a loaf of bread from the sideboard along with a small cup of mead on his way to his sire.

Stepping into the healing chamber quietly, he wasn't surprised to see his mother mopping Els's forehead. His father was trying to rearrange himself in his bed, cursing with every movement. He was in the actual bed in the chamber, with Els in the cot, small for him, but he probably was unaware of anything at the moment.

"Mama, I can watch over them. Get some rest." His mother stood and gave him a quick, forced smile, her eyes tired and slightly red. After all her years, Gracie Grant was still a beautiful woman. She had some gray mixed with her blonde strands, but unless you were standing in the sunlight, it was difficult to tell the difference. Her blue eyes held a sadness this morn, which he wished he could eliminate, but the only thing that would return them to their usual bright countenance would be for Els and Da to be hale again.

"I will go to my bed as soon as yer sisters come down. They promised to sit with them for a wee bit. Aunt Jennie should be here a bit after high sun, I hope. But she's getting on and doesnae travel as quickly anymore." Tears misted her gaze. "I must be prepared for her arrival."

"Mama, ye seem more frustrated than last eve. Aunt Kyla will prepare for Aunt Jennie. Dinnae worry about that. What is it that has ye upset?" His mother looked frazzled, which he didn't see often, especially in the healing chamber, though caring for his father couldn't be easy.

"Yer sire's leg. I keep trying to fix it, but 'tis

crooked. I cannae set the bone straight, no matter how hard I try. I know how it pains him. And yer brother continues to sleep no matter what I do. I need Jennie or Brenna or Brigid or Jennet…" She swiped at the tear on her cheek as angrily as he'd ever seen her do. "The bump on his head is no' going down at all."

He held his arms open, and his mother fell into them, crying quietly. His mother was as strong as anyone, but even she needed to let everything out once in a while. He whispered, "Aunt Jennie will fix them both."

"I pray ye are correct, Alaric. Please excuse me," she said, pulling back with a pat to his shoulder. "I'll go close my eyes. Come find me if either worsens. Aunt Kyla said she would bring in a platter of food soon."

He held out his piece of bread. "Eat it along the way, if ye please?" His mother was too thin, and he knew how stressful the act of healing was for her.

His father had always said that Jennie, Brenna, and Jennet were natural healers, but it wasn't that way for his mother. She struggled to be perfect. Aunt Ashlyn helped her many times, and so did Maryell and Merelda, but none came to it as naturally as it did to the other three.

"Many thanks to ye, Alaric." She left after she kissed his cheek, but then she paused at the door. "I know Aunt Jennie will help them."

No sooner had the door closed than his sire began to balk. "Gracie, come help me fix these blasted blankets, will ye, please? I cannae move them with my leg so fragile and my arm." His bed was positioned so he wasn't facing the door and hadn't noticed his mother leaving nor heard their conversation. Even that was unusual. His father had a second sense when it came to his mother.

Alaric set his drink down on the table in the center of the chamber, then took the stool next to his sire's bed. "I'll help ye, Da. I sent Mama off to bed. She's exhausted."

His father cursed and said, "I know she is. I tried to tell her to go earlier, but she's a stubborn woman."

Alaric arched his brow at his father.

"So I can be stubborn too. But ye better prepare yerself. Ye'll be taking my place soon."

That thought threw him, so much that his entire body jerked backward. It was several moments before he could reply. "I'm no' replacing ye. Da. Yer leg is broken, ye are nae passing on. Ye are still the chieftain. Ye and Uncle Connor. Yer wisdom is needed, no' yer leg."

Alaric stood and pulled the blanket clear off his father and worked to replace it more comfortably.

"Hmph," his sire grumbled. "I think 'tis time for new blood in the lairdship. We shall see." The man cursed three more times before Alaric managed to get the blanket arranged the way his sire wanted. "Mayhap my arm isnae broken. It feels better today."

"But no' yer leg?"

"Nay, my leg pains me something fierce. Even the blanket on it causes some pain. But I'm glad yer mother went to bed. She doesnae know how to straighten the bone and her attempts to fix it were killing me." He looked up at Alaric with a sheepish expression. "I tried no' to holler, but it was impossible. I fear I've hurt her feelings."

Alaric's mind was stuck on his father's previous comment. He was way too young to take over for his sire. Besides, everyone knew that it was Elshander's place to take over the chieftainship for his sire when he was ready to move on. Alaric didn't like the thought of becoming laird of Clan Grant.

Nay. Not for him. He was too young, too inexperienced.

"How is Els? Has he awakened at all, Da? Did ye hear him moan in the middle of the night?"

"Nay. He hasnae made a sound. Even when I was hollering at yer mother."

Alaric glanced over at his brother. There had to be something he could do to help him.

"He looks the same, but I'll see if I can wake him up at all. Mayhap he needs a loud voice to snap him out of whatever spell he is under."

His father glanced over at his eldest son, the sadness on his face evident. "He should have awakened by now. Tell me about the bump on the back of his head. Ye felt it before. See if it's shrinking yet. Yer mama says it must shrink before he'll awaken."

Alaric got up and moved over to his brother's bedside. He pulled a stool close, settling on it. He took in his brother's quiet breathing, pale color, and matted hair. Reaching for the back of his head, he decided the bump was too well hidden for him to see it clearly, so he turned his cheek to the side.

Els groaned but said nothing. Alaric froze, giving Els the chance to speak if he could, but he said naught.

His sire called out, "How does his wound look?"

"Not good, Da. 'Tis still partially covered in blood…"

"That doesnae matter, so Aunt Brenna told me once. I recall when Struan had one the size of half a walnut and it was soaked in blood. He could still talk. How big is it? 'Tis the important part of it."

Alaric probed through his brother's golden locks, finally finding the injury. The oval shape was nearly as big as a cow's full teat. "Papa, 'tis bigger than it was when I brought him in." It had definitely grown in the hours since he'd first noticed it.

"Pinch him. See if he reacts."

Alaric scowled. If he dared to pinch his brother at any time when he was hale, Els would have given him a quick punch in the belly. Pushing his stool back a wee bit, he pinched his leg.

Nothing. This time he tipped his head, peering at his brother to see if he was faking his sleep. That last pinch had to hurt. This time, he pinched his belly a little harder.

No reaction at all.

"He's no' feeling it, is he?" his father called.

"Nay, no reaction at all, Da. I'm sorry." He lifted one of Els's eyelids to peer into his deep blue eyes. He'd done this multiple times when they were young, and Els would jump at him. One time, Alaric had screamed like a lassie, and Els had fallen out of bed laughing.

Not this time.

The door opened, and Joya entered, carrying their youngest bairn, a wee laddie just a year born.

"Greetings to ye, Alaric. Has he awakened yet? Please give me some good news." Their son had his mother's red hair, sticking up in the middle of his head at present. He gnawed on a piece of crust.

He shook his head and stood. "Sorry, Joya. He's sound asleep. I just tried to wake him but he doesnae react."

She sat on the stool Alaric had just vacated and said, "I'll put his laddie on his belly. That may awaken him." Joya kissed Els on the cheek, then set the lad on his belly. "Come, Seamus. Wake up Papa."

The lad looked at his father's face, grinned, and leaned forward, tapping his chest and cheek. But Els did not react.

The door opened and his two sisters entered, Maryell and Merelda. The two were inseparable, and he was pleased to see them today.

"Mama went to sleep," he told them. "Wake her when Aunt Jennie arrives."

Then he left. It was just too disheartening to stay there.

How did healers go on so? Especially when the view was so dim.

He feared his brother would never wake up.

CHAPTER FOUR

ELI TOOK AIM, let the arrow fly, and hit the target. Then she shot another five in rapid succession. One hit the outside edge of the target, and she cursed. Loudly.

A curse she soon regretted because her grandmother appeared behind her on her horse. How had she been able to sneak up on Eli like that mounted?

"Uh-oh," she muttered, crossing her arms.

"Who are ye angry with?" Her grandmother climbed down off her horse and tethered him on a nearby bush. Eli hurried over in case she was unsteady, but she did fine this time.

"No one." She moved back to grab her bow and fired two more arrows, hitting the target square. "Why are ye here, Grandmama? I know 'tis difficult for ye with yer bad knees. Why no' stay inside?"

"Because I could see ye were upset. And ye are younger than that group of giggling young breasts in there."

Eli's shot went wide. "Grandmama! Giggling young breasts?"

"Aye. They are all the same age and ye are the youngest. I would guess they've teased ye a wee bit over the years. No one came to yer aid when they teased ye this time, so I came along. Keeps me busy. I dinnae like sitting around watching others."

Eli didn't know how to respond to that so she nocked another arrow and fired it. Hell, but her grandmother usually could judge a situation with uncanny accuracy.

"Nice shot," her grandmother said, sitting on a nearby boulder. "Who are ye mad at?"

"No one, Grandmama. Must I be angry to shoot well?"

"Nay, 'tis no' yer shooting that tells me ye are upset. 'Tis the speed at which ye raced out of the hall. I was just coming down the stairs when I saw ye leave. Someone say something they shouldnae have?" She crossed her arms, warming herself in the cool air.

"Nay, I'm fine."

"What were ye all talking about?"

Silence. Eli fired four more arrows—dead center—then retrieved them all.

"Did ye hear there is to be a patrol to the Borderlands?" her grandmother asked.

"Aye."

"Are ye going along?"

She sighed. "Aye." Then she returned to her spot. She was in no mood to discuss all that was said about Alaric Grant. She set herself and resumed her archery practice.

Her grandfather approached from behind them,

calling out to her grandmother. "Gwynie, I'm going to Bethia's to see how Thea and Willum are doing. Care to come with me?"

Her grandmother shook her head. "Ye go. I'll go on the morrow, Logan."

"While ye are here, convince this one to make an alliance for us." He gestured at Eli then turned his horse and left.

As her grandfather rode away, she nocked her arrow and aimed, peeking at her grandmother from the corner of her eye to see what her reaction was.

The older woman was staring at her, but now had changed her position and leaned forward, her head tipped down, taking on that expression she knew to be Gwyneth Ramsay suddenly understanding all that had happened.

Hellfire, but why did her grandparents have to be so quick in the mind?

"So Alaric Grant is going on patrol with ye, and yer grandsire wants ye to make an alliance by marrying him? And I will guess that ye arenae entirely fond of the man."

Alaric was a bit older than she was, though she had no idea how many years. But she was only eight and ten. He could be more than five and twenty winters.

Eli's next two arrows missed the target completely. Grandmama arched a brow and grinned. "I believe I have the answer to my question. Ye need no' say another word. I see ye dinnae like him at all."

Eli threw her bow down and stalked toward

her grandmother, her hands now fisted on her hips. "Why must Grandda butt into every part of my life? And why did he choose me to make the alliance? Ysenda could have married Alaric. And so could Ceit or Reyna or Isla. And what about Wenna? Why can he no' ask Wenna to choose Alaric? And if I do choose him, which I never will, but if for some reason it is forced upon me, then I suppose Grandda is going to tell me we need to have a bairn right away. And mayhap after that he'll ask me to ask the lairds to join the two clans. And then he'll want a second bairn, and a third until we get one of each, a lad and a lass. He'll have to have a chieftain and an archer, so I suppose I'll be big in the belly and ungainly for two years. Or will Grandda want me to be carrying all the time? Mayhap I willnae."

She crossed her arms and stopped in front of her grandmother, doing her best to calm her trembling lip.

She. Would. Not. Cry.

She never cried and she surely wasn't going to start over someone like Alaric Grant.

Her grandmother stood in front of her and whispered, "Ye dinnae need to do any of that if ye dinnae wish to."

"And Grandda willnae chase after me and tell me to do what he wishes?" One tear escaped, but she flipped her plait around, her tear flying off into the air in the process.

Her grandmother took her hand, unwound her crossed arms, and tugged her over to the boulder.

"Ye dinnae like Alaric?" The two sat on the boulder, and her grandmother faced her.

"Nay, I dinnae. He always tries to order me around. And then he teases me if I get angry. I prefer no' to be around him. Can ye no' convince Grandda to match Wenna with him? 'Twill never be me."

"Why do ye no' tell yer grandsire that yerself?"

"I did. I did in the hall, yet he comes here and tells ye to match us somehow. I dinnae like Alaric Grant, Grandmama. I dinnae wish to marry any man. I told them all I dinnae need a man and…" She looked away to hide the tears gathering in her eyes.

"And?"

"And they all laughed at me. And Reyna asked me if I knew what they meant and…"

"And ye didnae understand." Her grandmother slid over next to her and wrapped her arm around her shoulder. "Lass, things happen between a husband and wife. 'Tis all she meant. Lovemaking can be fun for some women. Some hate it, some love it. Did yer mother no' talk to ye about this?"

She shook her head, wiping away the tears she was unable to stop this time. "She tried a long time ago, but I told her I dinnae wish to know. I've heard other things, and I know most of it, but Reyna confused me."

Grandmama nodded. "I recall feeling the same. Ye shouldnae feel badly. They are all older than ye, and at the same stage in their lives. Lasses can be mean sometimes."

"So what do I do next time?"

Grandmother shrugged again and said, "When I was yer age, I told someone to stop talking or I'd put an arrow in their lips. I dinnae have a problem after that. If they're being rude, ye should be able to be rude in return."

Eli burst into laughter and hugged her grandmother. "Thank ye, Grandmama. But Grandda will yell at me if I do."

"Ye come see me if he does, lass." Grandmama kissed her forehead. "Men can be incredibly daft at times. Ye must learn to ignore them. Agree with them and ignore them."

"Truly?" Stunned by this answer, she couldn't believe her grandmother ever ignored her grandfather.

"How do ye think I've been able to live with Logan Ramsay all these years? I agree with him and ignore him. I do what I want, not what he wants. He thinks I listen to everything he says, but I dinnae. Never lose yer soul to a man, Eli."

"Grandmama!"

"I love Logan Ramsay for many reasons, lass. But he's no' my keeper. There's a difference. Now, I expect ye to keep this as our secret. Ye'll no' be giving my secret away to Grandpapa, will ye?"

She grinned and shook her head. "I promise."

"Come," Grandmama said. "Help this old lass get off the boulder."

Once she helped her to stand, she gave her grandmother a swift hug. "I do love ye, Grandmama."

"I love ye too, Eli. Do what makes yer heart sing, not what others tell ye to do." She walked across the meadow to her horse, then stumbled. "Hellfire!"

"Grandmama? What happened?" She hurried to her grandmother's side, not liking this at all.

"A hole in the ground. Deeper than usual. I'm fine, but my knee turned in an odd direction." She stood rubbing her knee. "'Tis a bitch getting on in years, Eli. Age isnae kind at all. I've had more trouble with my knees than I care to deal with. I hope ye have yer mind settled a wee bit. Dinnae be too angry with yer grandfather. He's just a crusty old curmudgeon. He'll always love ye. Never think otherwise."

"Are ye hale? Do ye need my help?"

"Nay, I can still make my own way. The day I cannae will be the day I move on. Fear no', I'm no' ready to leave yet. I love all my family and try to help where I can, but my eyes dinnae work as well as they used to. Ye still have good eyes. Use them."

"I will. Forgive me for all my complaining, Grandmama." Eli hung her head for all the anger she let out. "And I do love Grandpapa. I just dinnae always agree with him."

"Then ignore the stubborn old warrior. He'll get over it."

She giggled again.

CHAPTER FIVE

THAT NIGHT, ALARIC sat in front of the hearth after the evening meal, staring into the flames. His father was injured, and his brother would not awaken. He didn't like it at all. At least he knew his sire would heal. The broken leg would take a bit of time to heal, but his arm would heal quickly, or so he hoped.

Els? He had a sick feeling deep in his belly that his brother might never awaken. His mother had said she knew of a bairn of five or so who'd had the same type of fall. The child never awakened. Breathed well, she had said, but never awakened again. It was as if her soul was taken away. She'd never recovered, but her parents had taken her home and lovingly cared for her anyway.

Joya had two bairns to care for, and one was still wearing raggies.

What if his brother never recovered?

His father had already told Alaric that he might be taking over some of his chieftain duties for a short while. Hell, but he wanted no part of being chief of Clan Grant. There were too many people to keep happy, too many problems, and too many worries. Why the hell had he pushed everyone to take the shorter route? Because of the impending storm. But that storm had proven to be the cause of the injuries.

His cousin Broc joined him at the hearth. "Ye know 'tis no' yer fault, aye?" Broc was Alick's younger brother, just as Alaric was brother to Elshander. The three cousins, Alasdair, Alick, and Elshander had been born on the same day and had been inseparable their whole lives. Their younger siblings were close too.

"I suppose no'." He knew it wasn't his fault, but it sure as hell felt as though it was. Would they have taken the shorter route if Alaric hadn't suggested it? Els would have. His father wouldn't have. That was his guess.

Guess.

"Ye made the right decision, Alaric," Broc said. "Ye had to get the seed back. That was our first concern. Alick was yelling about it all the way back."

"I know. But if we'd just gone around…"

Broc refilled both of their ales. "If I had been in yer place, I would have done the same."

"Thank ye, Broc." Broc was one of his favorite cousins.

Els was heir to the chieftainship. What if he couldn't speak or walk?

The main door opened and three people entered the hall, shaking off their coats and knocking the mud from their boots.

Alaric jumped out of his seat, startled. He'd been so lost in thought that he hadn't heard them arrive. "Aunt Jennie, Uncle Aedan. I'm so glad ye are here."

Maitland came in behind them, closing the door behind him. "Alaric, Broc, how do ye fare?"

"We're fine, Maitland. But my father and brother did not fare so well."

"I brought one of the best to see if she can help." Maitland nodded toward their aunt, the youngest of the great Alex Grant's siblings.

Aedan set his hand at her lower back and ushered her to the end of the hall. "Come, Jennie. Sit by the hearth and warm up."

Broc rushed to get her mantle off, hanging it on a peg nearby.

Aunt Jennie glanced over toward the healing chamber. "I should probably check to see if Gracie needs me right away or not."

Alaric shook his head but said nothing, afraid to speak.

"What the hell does that mean?" Maitland asked, not moving from the spot he was in.

Uncle Aedan stopped and stared at him. "Did someone die?"

"Nay, nay." He ran both hands down his face, a sudden understanding of how his gesture could be interpreted. "Nay, Mama is waiting for Aunt Jennie to help her straighten Da's leg. Els hasn't awakened yet. So I doubt ye need to do anything right away. Allow me to get ye some wine from the cellar. Broc will see what food we have in the kitchens."

Aunt Kyla entered from the tower room. "I

thought I heard voices. Aunt Jennie, Uncle Aedan, 'tis so nice to see ye, and I thank ye for coming so quickly. Please sit by the fire, Auntie. Warm yerselves and I'll find something for ye to eat."

Maitland said, "Dinnae forget me, Kyla. I'm starving."

Alaric headed toward the kitchen just as Finlay entered, barking orders as he went. "Sit yer arse in that chair, Alaric. Tell yer aunt all ye remember about the accident. Broc and I'll help Kyla get the food. Aedan, are ye still able to handle the stairs? If so, I'll take yer bag above stairs once I return. Sit and rest yer bones after such a quick trip."

Alaric sat back down, grateful that Uncle Finlay had come along. He'd always been his father's second, and everyone adored him because he was so lighthearted. He could make anyone laugh over the oddest comments.

Uncle Aedan said, "We can both manage the stairs, Finlay. My thanks. I'm anxious for a wee sip of that amber liquid ye keep in the cellars. And Jennie would love a glass of wine to warm her insides."

Maitland took a seat after their aunt and uncle settled, while Kyla, Broc, and Finlay headed into the kitchens. Alaric reached into the basket by the hearth for a warm blanket and offered it to his aunt.

"My thanks to ye, Alaric. I will enjoy this. Now tell me exactly what happened in the accident. What did ye see of yer brother and father?"

Alaric explained how the accident took place,

but he didn't mention that he'd pushed them to go down the incline instead of the longer, safer route because of the weather.

If that wasn't a clear admission of guilt on its own. He feared he'd be blamed for the accident. He couldn't handle that on his conscience. His brother and his father both seriously hurt due to his careless actions.

"So Els landed on his head? Did he ever speak to ye after that?"

"Nay. He was fast asleep."

"And yer father. Gracie could not straighten the bone? I heard his arm was broken too."

Maitland chuckled. "I'm just going to suggest that Gracie didn't wish to set her husband's leg. I can picture Jamie fussing enough to unsettle her."

"It unsettles anyone to have to take care of a spouse. 'Tis so true," Aunt Jennie said with a grin. "My nephews are much like my brother Alex. Stubborn and bossy at times. I love them all dearly, but 'tis part of their nature."

Alaric, shocked, asked, "Grandsire? Bossy?"

"Och, aye. He was always bossing the four of us around when we were young."

Alaric knew she meant her sister Brenna and her brothers Brodie and Robbie. And his father did tend to boss his mother around at times. He had a sudden understanding of why his mother was so upset.

Kyla returned with a goblet of wine for Aunt Jennie, and Uncle Finlay handed all the men a wee bit of the *breath of life* while Broc set down a platter with a selection of cheese, berries, and a partial loaf of bread. Alaric stared up at his uncle, shocked to be handed such a treat with the adults.

"What? Yer sire never gave ye one? But ye are five and twenty. Well, I'm giving ye one. Ye look a wee bit too unsettled, Alaric. Ease yer mind. Whatever happened out there happened, and there's naught ye can do to change it. Take it in one swift gulp. Ye'll see."

Alaric had tried the golden liquid several times with his cousins, but his parents had never given him any. They considered it too precious to share with the younger group. In fact, the first time, Alasdair and Alick had drank almost all of it, leaving very little for him to taste. Maitland took his and swallowed a sip, smiling as he did so. "A fine batch, Finlay. I prefer to savor it."

Alaric decided to do what Finlay told him, so he swallowed it in one gulp, hoping it would calm him quickly.

And it did. He coughed a bit, the strange brew burning his throat, but within a few moments, a warmth washed over him. He couldn't stop the smile from spreading across his face.

"My thanks to ye, Uncle Finlay. 'Tis just what I needed." He held his cup out for more, but Finlay set it aside.

"No' yet. Let that first one settle on ye. Ye still must be able to answer yer aunt's questions, and this batch will put ye to sleep in no time."

Kyla brought out a tray of apple tarts. "Our fruit is nearly gone, Auntie, but these will serve for now. We're all praying for an early spring and a fine harvest."

"Have ye enough seed to plant?" Aedan asked. "We were thin, but I went to Inverness and traded for some oat seed and vegetables."

"Aye," Aunt Kyla said. "Jamie and the rest were returning from our neighbors after buying some seed from them. In fact, after we had everyone inside and in the healing chamber, it dawned on us that the seed they'd bought was probably ruined from the rain. But someone had the foresight to send the seed in right away."

Finlay reached over and patted Alaric's back. "Ye did some fine thinking. I heard 'twas ye who sent the seed in. Jamie was wild until he found out it was already inside. I checked it and all is fine but a small bag of turnip seed that was ruined. We'll be fine as long as our fields arenae flooded again."

"Or a drought," Aedan declared. "I heard Donnan has a fine setup, with his raised wood planters. Set above the ground, with holes in the bottom for the rain to drain. The man is mighty clever. I'm going to build some of my own, just in case we have another bad year."

"He did a fine job," Maitland said. "Saved enough seed to give us some bean seed. We are grateful."

Aunt Jennie stood up and folded the blanket she'd had on her lap. "The wine and the tart were perfect, but I wish to check on my nephews, if ye dinnae mind."

Aunt Kyla went with her, which gave Alaric the opportunity to talk to Maitland. "When do we leave on patrol?"

"I'll stay for one day, then Dyna and I will ride

out. Are ye staying back because of the accident, Alaric?"

"Nay," he said, a wee bit too quickly probably. "I'm concerned, but I agreed to go on patrol with ye, so I will do as I promised. There is little I can do here. I trust Aunt Jennie will get them both healed."

Maitland finished his drink. "And if she cannae help Els?"

Alaric let out a big sigh. "If she cannae do naught, what could I do? I'll go with ye. I honor my commitments."

He had to leave. If either of them took a turn for the worse, he'd never be able to live with the guilt. Keeping busy was the best thing for him.

Now, if he could only convince himself that their downfall was not his fault. He agreed with everyone who insisted it wasn't his fault, but in his gut, he felt differently. Their present state made him feel responsible, no matter what reason said.

Because if they were worse, he'd leave and never return.

CHAPTER SIX

⁓

ELI WOKE UP the next morn with an ache in her knee. She sat on the edge of her bed and rubbed her kneecap, trying to recall if the knee that hurt right now was the same one that her grandmother had hurt in the archery field.

Was this a true injury or was she taking on Grandmama's pain? How she hated the way it came on her at the oddest times. If it happened immediately, she'd have a better idea as to what the cause was, but it didn't always happen that way. Sometimes, the pain would start within a short time, but other times it could be the next day before her pain developed.

Fortunately, whenever she carried another's pain, it never lasted too long. She took care of her ablutions, dressed, and headed down the stairs. To her surprise, there was a huddled group of people toward one side of the hall. Some of the women were squatting on either side of someone Eli couldn't make out.

"Stand back, everyone. I'm fine." The voice sounded like her grandmother.

She approached the group and discovered it

was indeed her beloved grandmother the others were tending to. The dear woman was seated awkwardly on the cold stone floor.

"And dinnae get Logan. I dinnae want him here." She pointed at the group, circling her finger in warning.

Aunt Brenna sat on a stool next to her. "Gwyn, what happened?"

"I've always had trouble with my knee, Brenna. Ye know it. But I was walking yesterday and turned it. Overnight it blew up to this size. I dinnae know why it is so swollen. I attempted to walk across the room, and it buckled on me, so here I am. I cannae get up on my own."

Eli stepped closer, leaning over Ysenda's shoulder to see what exactly had happened. One look at her grandmother's knee made her gasp.

Ysenda looked at her. "What was that for?"

"Her knee. It looks so painful." Why the hell wasn't the woman writhing in pain?

"It is," her sister muttered with an extra hiss. "Hush now."

Eli was sick inside, wondering if her grandmother's knee had turned that badly because of the fall she'd taken on the archery field. A sudden feeling of guilt washed over her. Her grandmother shouldn't have come to the archery field, but she'd done it because Eli's cousins had teased her and she felt sorry for her.

She should have walked along with her to make sure she wasn't hurt.

"What is wrong with ye?" Ysenda asked, looking at her strangely. She tugged her sister over to the door. "Ye look as though ye are about to drop. Or is it cry? But ye never cry, so it cannae be that."

"I was with Grandmama at the archery field when she stumbled. Her foot caught in a hole. She said her knee took an odd turn. I'm feeling bad that she followed me there and now this happened." If she hadn't stormed off, her grandmother wouldn't have followed. She rubbed her cheek with the back of her hand.

"Stop doing that," Ysenda barked, grabbing Eli's hand away from her face. "'Tis no' yer fault. Ye didnae push her, did ye? Or dig the hole?"

"Nay, of course no'."

"Then 'tis no' yer fault. Stop wallowing. This is no' about ye."

Either way, she didn't wish to stay in the hall and watch her grandmother suffer. She had the answer to why her own knee had bothered her earlier, the burning inside so real. "I'm going to the stables to brush my horse down." She rubbed her knee to make sure it wasn't swollen.

"We'll talk later, Eli," Ysenda said, then headed back to the group helping their grandmother.

Eli couldn't get out of there fast enough, telling herself to stop limping just because she could feel her grandmother's pain as her own.

Her sire came toward her, her grandfather behind him. "Gavin, have a talk with yer daughter. I'm going to check on Gwynie." He moved past Eli without a glance.

She reminded herself that he was worried about Grandmama. That was the only reason he didn't speak to her. It was surely not because he was angry with her for not wanting to marry Alaric. Now she guessed she would have to listen to some lecture from her father.

Patrol was looking more and more inviting. Perhaps it was time to get away for a while.

"Eli, ye look upset. Did ye see Grandmama?" her sire asked.

"Aye, and her knee looks terrible," she said, rubbing her knee as if she spoke of her own.

"Are ye feeling the pain yerself again? I wish ye could control it, especially since it seems to happen more often now that ye are older." He motioned for her to follow him into the garden where there was a bench to sit on.

"I'll be fine. But Grandmama did step into a hole in the archery field yesterday and twisted her knee. I feel bad that it happened when she was with me."

Her father wrapped his arm around her shoulders and led her to the bench. "Now ye know Grandmama has had much trouble with her knee for a long time. Her pain has naught to do with ye."

"I hope no' or I would feel terrible. What did Grandsire wish for ye to talk with me about? Please tell me the subject isnae Alaric Grant again."

Her father broke into laughter.

"Why are ye laughing, Da?"

"Because 'tis exactly what he wants, an alliance with the Grants. He's hoping to tie one of his granddaughters up with Alaric. Yer grandsire thinks he's going to pass on someday soon and said he cannae leave until the alliance is settled. We cannae forget that he thinks he's running out of granddaughters of age. Brenna will be passing soon, so he wants a match in yer generation."

"Sometimes Grandda is daft," she whispered, peering over her shoulder after she said it. "He'll live forever, and ye know it."

"He's got some time, but unfortunately, he willnae be around forever. Now what is wrong with Alaric?"

"Naught is wrong with him, I just dinnae like him." She lifted her chin, hoping her words were the only thing her father required to believe her.

"Do ye know him well enough to be certain? He seems kind and honorable to me."

"Of course he is. He's a Grant, but he likes to order me around, and I dinnae like it. And why do men always like to order women around? Grandda does it all the time. I am old enough to make my own decisions."

Her father nodded slowly as he peered at her, his brow furrowed. "Ye are, I guess. Ye are eight and ten, so ye can think for yerself." He scratched his beard, assessing her carefully. "Ye are the youngest of my bairns, so I do forget that sometimes."

The entire situation with Alaric made her uncomfortable, but she'd feel the same about any man, she knew. "Da, I dinnae wish to marry. Must I?"

That comment surprised him, she could tell by his expression. "I suppose no', but why are ye set against marriage?"

"Because I dinnae like anyone enough to wish

to spend all my time with him. I've been around enough to know."

"Have ye ever been kissed, Eli?"

"Da!" She did her best not to blush, but she knew she had no control over it.

"'Tis a fair question. Ye need no' tell me who, just if ye have."

"I have. Many times."

He arched his brow at this comment but said nothing.

"I dinnae like exchanging spittle with a man. I see no reason to tie myself to one person. The prospect of living with a man, growing ungainly with bairns, then spending all my time taking care of them—I dinnae wish to do it."

"Ye dinnae have to. 'Tis what most lasses want as they get older, but no one will force ye to marry anyone."

"Promise? Ye'll no' let Grandda make me marry Alaric?"

"Nay, yer grandsire willnae force ye into any marriage. Ye are my daughter, and that decision is yers and yer mother's and mine. Why do ye worry about that?"

"Because I know I'm no' Grandda's favorite. He's always yelling at me. Now he's yelling at me to marry Alaric. Please ask him to stop." She bit back the words of anger that she'd love to unleash at her grandfather.

"Elisant Ramsay, ye know verra well that Logan Ramsay yells at everyone. 'Tis his way. He loves ye the same as all his grandbairns."

She didn't wish to argue with her sire. His

promise not to force her into marriage made her so happy that she didn't wish to ruin their time together. "I suppose so."

"I'd like to check on yer grandmother. Come with me. Ye'll see that she doesnae blame ye for her injury."

"Must I?" She'd rather not be forced to view the reminder of her grandmother's recent problems. She'd prefer to go to the stables or the archery field, away from where any feelings of guilt would assault her again.

"Aye, ye must. Ye'll be leaving on patrol on the morrow is my guess. And I dinnae wish ye to bear guilt that isnae deserved." He started to lead her back but then stopped in his tracks. "Ye do wish to go on patrol, do ye no'? Ye dinnae feel forced in that, do ye?"

"Aye, I do wish to go. I just dinnae wish to be forced into a relationship that isnae of my choosing."

"'Tis a foolish worry."

"Why is it foolish? He's told me, told Grandmama, and now ye." She had no idea why he would say such a thing. "He'll no' give up on it easily."

"Who is the one person that Grandpapa willnae argue with?"

"Aunt Brenna. Everyone knows that."

"And ye recall why?"

"Because she saved Lily and Torrian."

"And Uncle Quade. He was nearly dead when Grandda kidnapped her. And ever since then, he will not argue with her. But 'tis also because yer grandsire respects Aunt Brenna. He considers her to be wiser than any other person he knows."

"Besides himself?" she whispered.

Her father chuckled and said, "Besides himself. He thinks she has the wisest mind of all. I tell ye this because I think ye have the idea that Grandsire has a certain view of women. He does, but 'tis no' what ye think."

Now he had her totally confused. "I dinnae understand. What does he think of women?"

"Promise to never repeat this to him?"

"I promise." She had no idea what he was about to say.

"He believes women are stronger than men, and I cannae disagree with him."

"'Struth?"

"'Struth. And because he reveres Aunt Brenna so much, ye need no' worry about him ever forcing ye to marry."

"Why no'? What does Aunt Brenna have to do with my marriage?"

"Because Aunt Brenna's mother made Alexander Grant promise that he would never force any of his siblings into a marriage they didnae want. Elizabeth Grant was an unusual woman, and Aunt Brenna makes sure that no Ramsay forces a marriage on anyone either. 'Tis a private cause of hers. If she thought ye were being forced, she would stand up for ye."

"I'd heard that about the Grants, but I never knew why. 'Tis most interesting." She let out a large sigh. "And pleasing to know."

"Stop worrying about Grandda. Now, let's visit Grandmama."

She didn't relish going back inside, but she went along with her father. He'd just made her happier than anyone had in a verra long time, and she felt free to make her own decision. And no one would change her mind.

She was never getting married.

CHAPTER SEVEN

ALARIC SAT ON a stool next to his sire's bed in the healing chamber. "Does it feel better, Da?"

"Aye, once yer mother and Aunt Jennie straightened the bone, it took much of the pain away. And yer aunt splinted it tightly so I cannae move it much. I'll have the same contraption Ysenda used eventually, the kind that allows me to get around a wee bit, but for now, I'm stuck in this bed."

"I can carry ye into the hall if ye like."

"Connor and Magnus said they would bring me out for the evening meal. Gracie will hold the leg still while they move me. I have this bucket to pish in for now, but my pain is better. And I actually would like to sleep. The pain was fierce enough last night that I didnae sleep much. I promised Gracie I'd take a nap before this eve."

Alaric stared at his sire, trying to get the gumption up to say what needed to be said, knowing that it needed to be said now. He had to apologize, since the entire episode was his fault.

"Da, I'm sorry I led ye down the slope."

"Alaric, I would have suggested going that way if ye hadnae said anything. 'Twas more important that we get the seed into storage before the rain hit. We took a chance, and some of ye got through, just no' all of us."

Alaric thought for a moment. He hadn't been the first one through. Why hadn't he recalled that? He'd been about fourth in line, and they'd all been successful.

"The weather turning was what hurt us. Ye know it, but I do thank ye for having the presence of mind to send the seed ahead. If no', it could have been totally ruined. Finlay said it came through dry and will feed us well when the time comes."

The door opened and Uncle Connor came in. "Alaric, we're taking him out into the hall. He's been in here long enough. Will ye watch over yer brother while we carry him out?" Magnus entered behind him. "Gracie says he can nap near the hearth."

His mother came in last. "Jamie, do no' move that leg at all. I will move it."

"I know what to do, Gracie. Ye need to calm yerself."

The two bickered on as they often did, so Alaric turned his attention to his brother. He hated the sight of him so motionless and pale. Els did not look well at all. His mother kept changing his position, but he had yet to awaken.

Once the group left and he was alone with Els, and he knew this was time to speak to his brother. He had much he needed to say.

He sat next to his brother, setting the stool as close to his bed as possible, and he began his apology. "Els, forgive me for convincing ye to come down the incline. We should have gone around. What did it matter if we took the long way? It was the safest way." He stopped to swallow a few times. If not, he feared he'd cry like a bairn. "I know Da says I didnae make ye come that way, but I persisted when others suggested taking the long way. I shouldnae have been so pushy about it. I'll keep my mouth shut the next time." He knew what his father had said about many of them deciding the same, but it did not ease his guilt. He felt responsible, though his own sense of reason was beginning to flounder after speaking with his father. Perhaps it was not entirely his fault.

"Els, I miss ye." There. He'd said the words he wanted to say. "If ye can hear me, I beg ye to fight. Please try to wake up. We're all so worried about ye, but ye are my closest friend. Ye are my brother. I expected us to…" He stopped, wiping the tears from his eyes, not caring that he was crying. He needed to speak, because he believed his brother was still inside, that he could indeed hear him. "I expected us to grow old side by side, to marry beautiful lasses, have bairns who would grow up together. I wished to do the same as ye and Joya. I want my bairns to know ye as well as I know yours. Ye have to wake up."

He reached his hand behind his brother's head and felt the swelling still there. "'Tis no' growing any larger, and I think it may have shrunk a wee bit. So sleep until 'tis gone, but then ye must awaken. Mama is heartbroken and so is Da. And Joya, poor Joya tries to be positive around the bairns, but she's scared, Els.

"She's scared and so am I. And so are yer sisters and brother. Please wake up." He stopped again to wipe the tears from his face. "I need ye, Els."

The door opened and he quickly wiped his tears away. It was his mother.

"Oh, Alaric."

"I miss him, Mama. I just begged him to wake up."

His mother said, "Now that yer sire is out of the room, I'm free to do what I have longed to do since your brother came home." She pulled a stool over and lay her head on Els's chest and sobbed.

Alaric stepped away and let her cry her tears out, though he stayed nearby in case she needed him.

He'd cried his tears out; she needed her turn.

And while his mother cried, he prayed.

Eli tied her saddlebag to her horse, getting ready to leave with their small patrol group. The group from Clan Grant had arrived and were chatting in the yard, waiting for Eli, Tevis, and Wenna.

Wenna came in and said, "Are ye ready, Eli? I surely am. I wish to go south. Mayhap spring will be closer in the Borderlands. Are ye worried that our group is too small?"

"Nay, we have three archers and three

swordsmen. We'll be fine. I hope we find the English invaders quickly. I dinnae like to spend more than a moon on each patrol."

"I havenae been on many." Wenna leaned toward her. "So what do ye think of Tevis and Alaric. Do ye like either one?" Wenna had the long dark hair of her father. With her deep blue eyes, she was striking, especially because she was always smiling.

Eli didn't know exactly what Wenna meant by that so she was unsure how to answer. "I like everyone on the patrol, or do ye mean something more serious?"

"Aye. Do ye like either of them as a lad? Because I do, and I hope we arenae liking the same one," she whispered, glancing over her shoulder to watch for anyone entering the stable.

"I dinnae like either one like that, so ye may have yer choice. Which one is it?" Why was there a sudden squeeze inside her chest that said she hoped it was not Alaric?

"Tevis. I like Tevis. He kissed me once, and it was sweet."

Wenna was older than Eli, and it seemed she had more interest in men. Was Eli's sire right, and that was something that came with age?

Fortunately, Dyna entered, ending their conversation. But Eli was glad to know Wenna's interest. She would observe Wenna and Tevis along the way. This would prove interesting.

"Are ye ready, lasses? We're off to the Borderlands. Douglas says the English in Berwick Castle are starving and restless. He fears they'll be out in search of food soon. We're to go patrol along with Douglas and his men. There's a large area to cover."

"Does he think the English will be traveling as a larger group?" Eli asked. "We only met up with those few who tried going to market in Edinburgh last year. Mayhap they have gone elsewhere too."

Dyna shrugged. "Edward isnae sending any rations. Douglas said word reached him they've killed horses for food. They're in a desperate situation, for sure. They must send more out to search for provisions, but we dinnae know if they'll go in force or small bands."

Eli led her horse outside, grabbing some dried meat to take along, something they often kept in a bin for the stable lads. Food was still scarce after the famine last year. Clan Ramsay got by, as did most of their allies, but times would be tougher this year. Better to take a few provisions along than count on finding anything as they traveled.

Once outside, she nodded to Alaric. "I see ye are joining the patrol again, Grant."

"Aye. I hope we are successful. Even with our small group, we should be able to take any marauders down."

Aunt Brenna surprised her by coming out to greet those coming from Clan Grant. "Will ye come inside for a meal? I'd like to hear about yer sire, Alaric."

Maitland stepped in behind Alaric, joining the conversation. "Good morn, Aunt Brenna."

"Greetings, Maitland. I'm anxious for a wee update, if ye please."

Alaric replied, "We are stopping on Cameron land so we cannae stay, but I'm happy to update ye. My da is healing well now that Aunt Jennie has helped Mama set his leg. He sprained his wrist, and it will take time for him to be up and about, but he's adjusting. Magnus and Finlay move him, though he's no' the best patient when he's confined to a chair. But he's accepted his fate for now. I'm sure someone will be coming for that contraption Ysenda used, but he doesnae need it yet."

"And Elshander? I heard he had a severe head injury, Alaric."

"He has not awakened yet, Aunt Brenna. He's got a large swelling on his head. It has just begun to shrink. Think ye he has a chance at this point? I would love to hear yer opinion."

The look on Alaric's face struck Eli. His pain washed through her as if it were her sister Ysenda hurt again. When Ysenda had broken her leg in the avalanche, Eli had been distraught, but at least a bone could heal. Elshander's situation sounded much more serious.

"He took a bad fall?" she asked, wondering why she hadn't heard the news. Or had she? So worried about her grandmother, she hadn't paid much attention to anything else. She chided herself for being too focused on one thing, promising herself to pay better attention to those around her.

Dyna explained. "Uncle Jamie and Elshander

both. Their horses fell coming down a slope slick with rain. Els landed on his head. The blow knocked him out, and he hasnae awakened yet. Uncle Jamie landed on his leg and is healing."

Aunt Brenna took Alaric's hand and squeezed it. "I've seen similar head injuries many times. There have been situations when the injured is out for a sennight. One was out for nearly a fortnight, and he still awakened. He lost some of his thinking ability, but he came to and was able to speak just fine. But some never awaken either. I pray that Elshander will awaken and be hale."

"Thinking ability?"

"Much like an apoplexy, an injury to the head can cause some strange things to happen. He could have trouble talking. He could lose some memories or just not be able to work out puzzles as well. Sometimes physical abilities will be affected as well. I dinnae understand how the brain works, but with time, some of the loss can sometimes return. For others, the loss can be permanent. But remember, Elshander could awaken tomorrow and be perfectly fine, especially since he's a young man in his prime. Ye must have faith. Give my love to my sister when ye see her, please."

Aunt Brenna gave Alaric a tight hug and returned to the keep, stopping once to turn around and say, "Godspeed to ye all."

Eli was sobered by the news, especially for Alaric. "I'm sorry to hear about yer brother and father, Alaric. 'Tis a most difficult situation." Two in his close family were stricken. For her, just the incident with her sister had upset her terribly.

And now her grandmother was ailing. Would it never cease? She couldn't stop thinking about her grandmother, and her situation wasn't nearly as bad as Alaric's brother or father. How was he handling everything so well?

"My thanks," Alaric said, a heavy sigh telling her exactly how he felt. "I'm going to believe Els will awaken. 'Tis my hope." Alaric mounted and turned his horse toward the path, the others following.

Little as she liked him and even less the idea of marrying him—no matter what her grandsire said—this sad turn of events changed her whole demeanor toward Alaric.

She'd have to be kind to him.

She'd rather tell him to kiss her arse.

CHAPTER EIGHT

HAVING ELI AS part of their patrol was probably the only good thing in Alaric's life at the moment. He expected her sparring banter, though he wasn't in the mood for it. Even so, her company made it harder to wallow in his worry and guilt.

They'd traveled three hours south without event. Maitland and Dyna rode in front while Tevis rode next to Alaric in the back, behind Wenna and Eli.

Exactly where he didn't wish to be.

He experienced an entirely unexpected response to seeing the sweet arses in front of him. He had to force his gaze away from Eli's exquisitely formed bottom. He'd never anticipated *attraction*. He'd thought to enjoy their trip together, but not this much and not in a way that forced him to rein in his thoughts so as not to embarrass himself.

Eli Ramsay was proving to be a saucy lass without doing anything at all.

He recalled his cousins chatting with his brother a few years ago about a lass's bottom when riding a horse. They'd chuckled about one lass in particular, though Alaric couldn't recall which one. They'd made various facial expressions along with the accompanying noises to express their opinion on said arse—lip smacking, tongue wagging, and kissing motions, among others.

Alaric had thought they were all losing their minds. Why would anyone wish to truly kiss anyone's arse? Elshander had chuckled when he'd asked him that question once they'd been alone. Els had ruffled his hair and said, "Someday ye'll see, lad."

He hated to admit that his brother was right. Oh, he'd admired the sweet curves of many lasses in the past. But this was different. This was more than just a passing glance, a quick peek. It wasn't because he was older either, it was because of who had caught his attention.

Eli was different.

Tevis must have noticed, because he laughed. "Ye are sweet on her, I see. Think ye she feels the same?"

He glared at Tevis. "Nay. And nay!" Perhaps he'd been a bit too loud voicing his denial because Tevis laughed harder.

"Sure ye dinnae. I know what I see."

"Think what ye wish, but I know whose arse ye are looking to caress," Alaric grumbled. He'd noticed where his friend's gaze had drifted, and it wasn't to the birds over their heads.

"I'll no' deny it one bit," Tevis said, nodding his head. "I hope she allows me close enough someday."

Wenna glanced back over her shoulder at Tevis and blushed.

Alaric shook his head. The girl's hearing was amazing.

Maitland pointed to a spot off the main path. "That way. We'll take a brief respite before continuing. I think it might be better if we split up. But we'll eat and discuss it."

They arrived in the clearing, Alaric glancing up at the gray clouds that were beginning to cover the sky. They'd had a bit of sunshine, but it was disappearing and promising to give way to the usual cloud cover. At least it was not raining.

Spring was showing itself everywhere. Some trees had begun to bud, and he'd seen a few flowers poking up through the leftover snow crystals in spots. He was more than ready for summer. Enough of the cold and the ice. They needed warmth, especially for the trees to blossom so they would bear fruit, though it would be a long time yet. It was nearly time to plant the few fields they had left from last year's floods.

Spring was the sign of new beginnings, and he looked forward to it every year.

Except this year.

His father's and brother's injuries overshadowed everything. It was as if someone threw a shroud over the entire clan, their daily interactions all subdued and tainted with a worry that he hated. Until Els woke up and Jamie was riding his horse again, the clan would not change.

Nor would he. The first thing he thought of every day was the health of his brother. He knew his sire would heal, but no one could tell him anything about Els. No one could predict if he would ever awaken.

Not Aunt Jennie, Aunt Brenna, his mother, or any other healer he knew.

As soon as they gathered, Maitland headed into the bushes, so he pulled Dyna aside and asked, "Any visions of my brother yet, Auntie?" Dyna had a sound reputation as a seer.

"Nay. They may come to me at any time, or I could learn something in a dream when I'm sleeping. But I've seen naught about Els yet, Alaric. I'm sorry." She shook her head and set her hand on his forearm. "If I do, ye will be one of the first I tell. Trust me that I willnae forget."

He nodded and grabbed a piece of dried meat and sat down on a log. Once Maitland returned from his visit to the trees, they all gave him their attention.

Dyna chewed on a piece of cheese and asked, "How do ye wish to split up? That is, if ye still believe it to be the best way. 'Twould definitely cover more ground, though it comes with risks."

Maitland glanced up at the clouds and then said, "I think we could do this quicker if we split up. I dinnae like the clouds rolling in. There are six of us. Easy enough at the upcoming split in the path. There are three different ways, and all three end at a crossroads about an hour's ride farther on. If we split into pairs, we can each take a path."

"Where do they head?" Tevis asked.

"The Borderlands, which is our destination. Sir James Douglas, warden of the marches, is determined to protect his march. The two outside paths are commonly used by reivers hoping to avoid anyone who might be on the main road. Since we haven't seen many travelers, I think we're safe in splitting up. What say ye?"

"Aye," Alaric offered. "Tevis and I can take one path."

Maitland and Dyna both stopped eating and shook their heads.

"No' how it works," Maitland said. "One archer and one swordsman. Ye will go with Eli, and Tevis will go with Wenna. Dyna and I will take the main path, the place we're most likely to meet anyone. It forks a second time, briefly, so we can split and look for any English soldiers scavenging for food."

"They are most likely to be on the main path," Dyna said. "They willnae know yer paths well. But be careful if you come upon anyone."

Alaric accepted his assignment without argument. They'd seen little traffic, so he wasn't worried. An hour alone with Eli would be easy enough to handle. She'd curse him out a hundred ways, but that he could listen to, no matter where they were. Bantering with Eli might keep his mind from going back to his brother.

They finished their meal in pleasant companionship. Before they rode on, Maitland called their attention back to him.

"A word we must agree upon. The paths split but we should be rejoined in less than an hour and a half. If anything happens, meet back here whenever ye can. Get away from the path if ye see numbers too large for ye. If we don't all come to the crossroads within an hour and a half, whoever is there should wait a quarter hour, and if anyone is still missing, take their path back here."

Dyna added, "And know that we will only travel on the main path after this. We'll no' split up again."

Alaric thought that made perfect sense. His sense of direction was not the best. His brother liked to tease him that he could get lost in a large stable. That jest had been the cause of many brotherly fights.

But put Alaric in an unfamiliar area, and he couldn't argue with his brother's teasing. Every patch of forest or hillside looked the same to him. His sire always told him to watch for landmarks, but one tree looked just like the next. A clear path should be all right, though.

They made it to the point where they were to split up and headed off in different directions. Tevis and Wenna to the left while he and Eli took the right path. They were headed southwest, or so he was told. He had no idea.

Neither spoke for the first ten minutes. But then he couldn't stand the silence. "Are ye angry with me for some reason?"

"Nay," Eli said, peeking over at him. "No' mad about anything."

"How do ye wish to pursue this?"

"What the hell does that mean?"

"Do ye want to ride fast? Slow? We both look

at both sides or ye just to yer left and I to my right? Or what the hell, we could just watch the sky for any bird about to land white shite on us."

"Verra funny," Eli mumbled. "Stay at this pace. I'll look left. Ye to the right."

They continued, still not conversing, but the sky began to darken in a way he didn't like. He glanced up at the rolling clouds, not surprised to see some black clouds approaching.

"Hell, I hope 'tis no' about to rain."

"I hope no' either. I hate damn rain, especially when it comes down so hard that it looks like shite slanted in the distance. The kind that hits ye right in the face like a ruffian would."

"Do ye always curse so?" Alaric noticed Eli saved her cursing for when she was not in a crowd or a group. He guessed with just the two of them that she'd unleash a few more obscene oaths before she was finished.

She never answered, instead focusing on the task at hand. Ten minutes later, Alaric could smell the storm in the air, and the black clouds were nearly over them.

"Do ye know the area, lass? Is there somewhere we can shelter until the rain ends? It could be just a quick storm, but 'twill be a storm, no doubt."

"Nay, I dinnae know the area at all."

"But ye are a Ramsay."

"And so I'm supposed to know every area? Ye do know how big this forest is? Or do they no' teach ye such things on Grant land? Or are yer forests minuscule?"

"Verra funny, ye are. We are closer to Ramsay

land than Grant land. I simply wondered if ye know the land better than I do." As soon as he finished his sentence, the clouds opened, drenching them. It felt as though they were being pelted by hail from all four directions.

"Find us somewhere, ye fool!" Eli's voice carried in the wind, including the bite.

"Fool?" Alaric had his hand in front of his face in an attempt to protect his eyes from the stinging raindrops. "Ye wish me to help but ye call me a fool? Find yer own place to hide."

Alaric led his horse off the path to an area thick with pines, one way to stay out of the rain. He made his way into the copse, but the rain was so hard, the branches didn't do much good. The ground was rapidly turning into a muddy, boggy mess.

"Hellfire, we need to find somewhere."

Eli was right behind him, cursing all the way. "God's bollocks!"

"What the hell! Dinnae take God's name in vain like that! He'll make us both pay."

He led his horse forward, no idea where he was headed. He hoped his horse had some instinct that would help find some kind of shelter. Making his way slowly forward, he wished he'd packed more clothes than the one change he had. The rain was relentless, drenching, and the kind that cooled the air. He shivered and pulled his wool plaid closer about him.

"There," he said, pointing ahead. "A small cave, but big enough for the two of us."

She nodded. "Hurry up!"

Alaric wished to tell her to shut up. And as soon as they were safely ensconced in somewhere dry, he would.

CHAPTER NINE

HELL, BUT HOW had she gotten stuck with the fool of Clan Grant? Stuck in a muddy pool of rain, Eli dismounted, tugging on her horse's reins to get him to move forward. He didn't like the flooded mess they stood in any more than she did.

Alaric had miraculously found a cave, and it was a bit above the ground, so at least they wouldn't be stuck in a gully full of raindrops. They headed toward the cave, and once he had his horse tethered safely, he returned to help her, taking her reins and tugging the beast into a spot that shielded the cave opening from much of the rain. He was able to let enough of the reins out to give them enough space to stick their heads inside the cave.

She grabbed her saddlebag and raced into the cave, and once Alaric had her horse tethered next to his, he did the same, though the area he'd found, even outside the cave, was much better than standing in the worst of it. Both animals turned their heads toward the cave, shielding themselves from the worst of the onslaught. She noticed him talking to his mount before giving it a kind pat on its flank. His words carried through the rain.

"We'll be back. Ye'll be fine here."

So the man did have some finer points to his personality. Kindness to animals definitely counted with her.

Inside the cave, she fell onto a boulder just inside, wringing the rain from her hair the best she could. Then she searched inside her saddlebag for a linen square to dry her face and for a dry tunic.

She stepped into the back of the cave where it was dark, tore off her wet tunic, then quickly put the fresh one on.

"Warn me next time, Eli. For Heaven's sake, ye are nearly naked."

She sighed, arranging herself so she was presentable. "Then stop looking. 'Tis only a bare back. Why would it bother ye? Do ye wish for me to turn around instead?" It wouldn't bother her at all, though she was one of the few lasses who felt that way. What did she care if a man saw her breasts? They were just two blobs meant for a bairn's mouth. As far as Eli was concerned, they only got in her way, especially when nocking an arrow.

He spun on his heel and faced out, looking through the deluge to the landscape. "I wonder where the others are."

She'd been thinking the same. "We're supposed to meet within the hour. If we stay here, will they leave without us?"

Alaric said, "If I know Dyna, she'll be hiding in a dry place. She doesnae like rainstorms either. I dinnae know Wenna and Tevis well enough to know if they would continue or if they would do the same as us. But I'm no' taking my horse out in that. Look at them. They are both turning away from the rain. It reminds me of when my sire and brother took their falls. Both of their horses slid in a wee bit of a mudslide. Look at them now. 'Tis no' safe out there."

Eli couldn't imagine what it would be like to watch someone get hurt like that. "I hope yer brother heals."

"Many thanks. So do I."

The rain didn't last long, so as soon as they thought the area was dry enough and the rain off for good, they left, heading back toward the path they were on. There was only one problem.

Where was it?

The rain had washed away all signs of their passing, and a mist had developed, swirling low enough to obscure their vision as the horses moved forward. At one point, Eli's horse decided it was not interested in going any farther. The air was sodden and clammy, the cold reaching its damp tendrils deep into her belly.

She wanted to go home. A sudden bad feeling crept up her back and her neck, making her shiver in the cooling evening air.

"The path is gone." Alaric stopped and dismounted, handing the reins of his horse to her. "Let me check the area."

For a moment, he disappeared into the mist,

and she couldn't wait for him to return. He reappeared, then went in a different direction, then reappeared and chose a third direction.

When he returned, he stopped in front of her and said, "I have no idea where we are. I expected the path to be not far, but I cannae locate it. Do ye recall which way to go?"

"Nay," she said, suddenly skittish about the entire situation. "I dinnae know the area and I'm no' good with directions."

He chuckled. "I'm worse with directions. We'll remember that the next time we break into groups or pairs. We shouldnae be together. Until then, what do we do?"

"We'll guess. Which way do ye think would be the best? I'll count to three and we'll both point and see if we agree."

He crossed his arms and said, "As good as anything I could think of."

"Ready? Then one, two, three!"

Oddly enough, they both pointed in the same direction. She smirked and said, "Get yer arse in the saddle and let's go. I wish to be with the others before nightfall. No offense to ye intended."

"Understood. I prefer to be with a larger group too." He swung onto his horse and said, "Come on, Midnight Blue. Take me to Dyna and Midnight Shadow."

They headed off, staying as close together as possible. The air was as still as ever, so they had no trouble hearing each other.

She finally asked, "Why the name for yer horse?"

"No one gets it except Grant mounts. They are all descendants of Grandda's horse, Midnight, a brilliant black warhorse who carried Grandda in the Battle of Largs. My grandfather adored him, so he had the stallion stand with many of the clan's best mares. Thus, many of his foals carry his name in some way. We have Midnight Dancer, Blue, Ray, Shadow, Moon. A couple of people call them by number, but I cannae do it that way. Numbers dinnae help me in the least."

"I love numbers. Not a surprise, since we are opposites in many ways."

"But ye dinnae call yer horses by number."

"Nay, his name is Moonlight. Names suit me fine."

They rode on in silence for another half an hour before she stopped her horse, dread pooling in her belly. "Alaric, we should admit it—we're lost."

"Mayhap no'. The path could be just ahead."

"Call me a witchin' bitch if ye want, but if ye look there, ye'll see a small loch up ahead. I dinnae recall ever seeing a loch before." She pointed straight ahead, and Alaric moved his horse for a better view.

"Shite if ye arenae correct." He turned his horse to look at her. "We're lost."

"Ye hedge-born fool, I just told ye that. Do ye never listen?"

"I'm no' hedge-born and ye know it. I'd appreciate it if ye'd stop insulting me."

"I only insulted ye once."

"True, and ye insulted yerself, too. What the hell is a witchin' bitch anyway? I've no' heard that expression before."

"I made it up, arsehole."

"Now I'm an arsehole? I might just take my leave. Ye'd prefer to be alone, it sounds like to me."

"I dinnae care what ye do. Go ahead and go." Hellfire, but she'd never admit the truth of their situation. Her feelings for this brute had grown tenfold just from being stuck in the rain with him. And the last thing she wished for was to be lost by herself. He'd better not leave her here alone, or she'd chase him down and curse at him for days. She dared to peek at him, at his broad shoulders and his handsome face, even with the stubble growing. And if she were to guess, it was coming in a shade of red, unlike the blond hair on his head.

She had to stop staring at the man.

"Hell nay, I'm no' going anywhere without ye. Do ye think I'd leave ye here to fend for yerself? Do I look like a fool? If I left ye, yer grandfather would hang me by my bollocks somewhere."

"Nay he willnae. He doesnae care anything about me. Believe me, I'm naught special to him." She could still see that look of disdain in his eyes when he walked past her to go into the keep, blatantly ignoring her. What grandparent ignored their granddaughter? Only Logan Ramsay and Elisant.

"Then we have something in common, because no one will care that I'm no' returning."

"Ye are still spitting slime out. Ye are a Grant.

Isnae yer mother Kyla Grant? The firstborn daughter of Alex?"

"Nay, my sire is Jamie, and my mother is Gracie."

"Och, ye are the son of the chief and no one will miss ye? Ye are full of shite, Alaric."

"The hell I am. After what I've done, no one will care if I return."

She couldn't believe what he said was true, but it felt so good to argue with the man that she couldn't stop herself. "What the hell did ye do to pish everyone off?"

He dismounted and began to pace in a circle. "'Tis my fault my brother and father got hurt. And my brother may never wake again."

"At least they liked ye before. My clan has never liked me."

"What the hell are ye speaking of? Ye are Ramsay blood. Yer grandmother would spit fire for ye."

"She might, but my grandsire wouldn't. The last time I walked past him, he didnae even speak."

He moved over to stand in front of her horse, his hands on his hips. "Ye are lying."

"Nay, I'm no'. I've always been a disappointment to him. I've never been as good an archer as my cousins. No matter how hard I try, I can never match them. And what do ye mean that ye caused the accident? Did ye push them off their horses?" She was yelling at the start, but the last part came out barely audible.

He couldn't be serious.

"Nay, I didnae push them, but we had two choices on our return to the keep. We had seed we'd purchased from our neighbor, and we could see a storm was nearly upon us, so I pushed to take the shorter route. It was riskier because it could be treacherous for the horses in the rain, but I thought we could beat the storm. Only a few of us made it down the slope before the rain started. My father's horse and my brother's horse both lost their footing. It was awful."

"I'm sorry. That must have been hard for ye to watch. I know…"

"How do ye know?"

"Because I watched my grandmother take a fall when she twisted her knee the other day. If I hadn't left the keep alone, she'd no' have followed me. It was my fault she fell."

"Och, so ye pushed her?" His grin told her he was teasing her the same way she'd teased him.

And when had Alaric Grant become so handsome? His hair was just beginning to dry from the rain, but she noticed something else about him that she had never noticed on anyone before.

His tunic melded to his muscles, and he looked quite fine.

She was losing her mind for sure.

They were lost and had no idea how to get back to the path. She was starving and there was little for them to eat.

But she had an urgent need to run her hands up Alaric's chest and then nibble on his lower lip.

She was surely turning into a witchin' bitch. A slutty one at that.

CHAPTER TEN

ALARIC HAD TO turn away from Eli before his erect member gave him away. Hell, but did she have to look at him that way—that way that ended with her licking her lower lip slowly while she stared at his chest?

If that look didn't rouse his need, nothing would. Her green eyes had the longest lashes he'd ever seen on anyone. Hell, he'd never noticed anyone's eyelashes before. Her skin carried a light bronze from the sun with a smattering of freckles across her pert nose. Her hair looked brown some days and blonde on others, as if someone gave her hair two different colors and mixed all the strands. It was neatly plaited before the storm, but many strands had escaped since then and framed her face with a slight curl. None of that enticed him like the rest of her. The pink lips were just the right size of plumpness, and the curves she carried were unmatched.

She was nearly perfect in his eyes.

He looked off into the distance, not surprised that he couldn't see far at all. But someone had to make a decision. It might as well be him.

"All right. I say we return to the cave for this eve. We cannae ride in the mist for hours—we might never find our path again. In the cave, we can get a good night's sleep, even if it rains again, and wake up refreshed and able to find our way back on the morrow. As it is, I think we've circled about for more than two hours. Mayhap the mist will be gone in the morn."

Eli didn't say anything, just stared up at the sky. In fact, he thought her eyes were growing wet.

"Dinnae cry, Eli. I'll protect ye."

"Cry? I never cry. What made ye ask me such a ridiculous question? What the hell have ye been thinking? I agree with yer suggestion. I dinnae like to sleep on sodden ground. I have to be dry, which also means no raindrops falling from treetops. I'll never sleep on the ground, wet as it is after that storm. Lead the way."

"Me?" Hell, but he didn't know if he could do it. He mounted his horse and swung its head to point—he hoped—back the way they'd come.

"Aye. Ye know the way, do ye no'?"

Nay, he surely did not, but he wasn't about to admit that to her. "Of course. That way." He turned his horse but he heard a shout behind him.

"Nay, that way. God's bollocks, do ye no' know anything?"

He covered his ears. "Will ye please stop with the blasphemous cursing? Just say hell or hellfire or bollocks even, and leave God out of it."

She sighed. "I'll try my best. Hellfire," she drawled. "Do ye no' know anything? We have to go that way." She pointed in a different direction.

"Do we? Are ye sure?" He was more confused than ever, but when the fog was so thick that the sun was hidden, it was difficult to judge directions. His cousin Alasdair knew where he was without ever checking the sun. How Alaric wished he were with them now.

Alaric could hardly find the sun.

"All right. We'll go that way."

They had to adjust their directions on three different occasions, but they finally found their way back to the cave. "Yer horse is a better guide than ye are, Grant."

Alaric barked out a chuckle. "I cannae argue with that, but ye arenae much better, Ramsay." He winked at her.

"Dinnae wink at me." Her lips made a straight line that was surely the biggest pout he'd ever seen.

He did his best no' to laugh at her, though it would be better if he laughed than if he told her exactly what was going through his mind. She was cute when she looked annoyed. He was going daft, for sure. That was it.

"All right. I'll never wink again. I beg yer pardon, lass. But only if ye quit the blasphemy."

She narrowed her gaze at him but said nothing.

After settling their horses, they found their way into the cave, Alaric making sure to follow Eli so he could look at her sweet arse. He would die before ever admitting such a scheme to her, of course.

She was a prickly sort, but he liked that she kept him alert, so to speak. He'd never dare to fall asleep around her because she'd do something like his brother and cousins used to do.

Comb his hair in a different way.

Paint his face with ashes.

Put a foolish hat on his head.

Once they carried him outside, and he never awakened until they yelled at him with swords aimed at his belly.

Once they put his hand in a bowl of water because someone told Els he would wet his bed if they did it.

Fortunately, he proved his brother wrong.

He let out a deep sigh, hoping he'd have the opportunity to argue with his brother again. He enjoyed their banter, just like he enjoyed bantering with Eli. It was a challenge, and it kept his mind off other topics.

Like his brother and his father. Like how much he'd failed them both.

"Stop whining."

"I'm no' whining." His hands went to his hips. How could she call what he was doing whining? He hadn't made a sound.

"Aye, ye did. Ye were sighing. Nearly the same as whining."

And suddenly, Alaric was tired of arguing. "I'll do my best. Look, I'm tired and I'm sure ye are the same. I have some dried meat I can share and a hunk of cheese. Then I'm going to try to get some sleep."

Eli said, "I'll go along with that plan. I'm verra tired too. I have a wee bit of dried meat left too. My apologies for being so abrupt. I'm worried.

I just hope we can find our way back on the morrow." She plunked down on the boulder and took the proffered hunk of cheese, biting into it slowly.

"We will. Once the mist is gone, we'll be able to see the landmarks to guide us. If ye cannae see in front of ye, finding a path will never be easy. 'Tis annoying that the weather has made it so difficult. But at least we havenae fallen because of an avalanche. We've no' been attacked like poor Thea. Not been kidnapped like Reyna. Not locked in a cellar like Isla and Grif. And at least this cave is big enough for both of us. There's a wee bend to block the wind. I think we should sleep back behind it."

Eli smiled. "I am shocked when I consider all that has happened to our friends and clanmates on patrol. I'm glad I missed much of it. Are ye worried about the English finding us?"

"Nay," he replied. "The issue with Thea was vengeance for stealing their quarry and later, wounding one of them."

"The one Englishman was apparently offended that a lass struck him with an arrow. I'd like to be the one to hit him, if that were the case."

Alaric laughed. "Aye. This patrol will be more interesting, if the English really are coming out in force. Dyna thinks there will be a true battle. Have ye been in battle yet?"

"Nay. I must admit it makes me a wee bit anxious thinking on it. I am no' sure how well I can handle looking at dead bodies. Have ye been in a big battle?"

"Nay, no' yet." He chewed on his dried meat, finishing up the last piece. "We have to find our way out on the morrow. We'll run out of food soon."

"We can both hunt. We'll no' starve, Alaric."

"I know. But I hope to catch the group. This isnae what I thought I'd be doing on patrol."

They finished their meager meal and readied for the night. Alaric knew the night would be cold but how exactly did one suggest sleeping together for warmth to someone like her?

"Ye can sleep close to me if ye'd like my heat, lass. I promise to be honorable."

"If we do, we'll end up like Brin and Ceit. 'Tis what they did in the cold, or so I heard."

"Wagging tongues like to tell stories. Ye have my word as a Grant warrior that I'll be honorable."

"I'll be fine, Alaric. My thanks for offering. I'll sleep deeper into the cave. I dinnae want some odd creature coming up to me in the middle of the night."

"Fine. I'll gladly sleep closer to the mouth. I hate spiders, so I dinnae wish to sleep in the back of the cave."

"Afraid of spiders? Truly? Why?"

"Probably because my brother and cousins used to hold me down and tease me with them. Now I hate all spiders."

"Now that was just cruel," Eli said. "Ye may have the front of the cave." She rubbed her cheek, a nervous habit if he were to guess.

Alaric settled once he knew she'd found her spot, then crossed his arms, his head on his spare plaid, which had finally dried from the rain. They weren't that far apart, close enough for him to keep watch over her. His grandfather's teachings told him that he was responsible for the lass whether she liked it or not.

He closed his eyes once he knew she'd settled, then cleared his head so he could sleep. The only thought in his mind was a lass with long brown hair, green eyes, and an unusual vocabulary of curse words.

Someday he'd like to kiss the curses off her tongue.

CHAPTER ELEVEN

WHEN ELI WOKE up, it was pitch black outside the cave. In fact, it was so dark that she couldn't tell exactly where the mouth of the cave was. A light snoring told her where Alaric was, and something else caught her attention.

She was frozen. Not truly frozen, but she would be as cold as the top layer of ice on a loch soon enough if she didn't do something about it.

She'd heard her cousins often jest about their husbands being as hot as a hearth and that it was one of the finer things of marriage, but she never actually believed it. But apparently, every bit of it was true.

She shivered, the cold from the stone floor and the one plaid she had sending tremors through her that she couldn't stop. Edging her body closer to Alaric bit by bit, she hesitated every time his breathing changed because she didn't wish to awaken him.

She just wanted his heat. How close would she have to get to him to absorb some of his warmth? She'd take any wee bit he could share with her.

After shimmying across the stone, she reached a spot where she could reach out and touch his back with her fingers, and she sighed, basking in the warmth that emanated from him. How the hell did men do it?

She had to learn this trick. Until then, she'd take whatever Alaric was putting off. Closing her eyes, she moved just a wee bit closer, smiling as the wave of body heat hit her.

"Lass, no reason to sneak. All ye have to do is ask."

Her eyes snapped open. He rolled over to face her, a slight grin on his face, the stubble on his cheeks making him look even more handsome.

"Come closer. I'll no' touch unless ye ask me to."

She slid closer, letting out a small moan of pleasure when there was little space between them.

"Keep making that sound and there will be trouble." His arched brow told her he meant what he said.

She glared at him and snuck her feet closer to his legs.

He whispered, "Take yer boots off."

"My feet will freeze," she whispered, though she didn't know why. There was no one around to overhear them.

"Nay, I'll warm them. I've heard a lass's feet will be the coldest. True?"

"They are cold, but removing my boots will make them colder."

"Ye willnae know until ye try, will ye?"

His hand came across and found hers under the plaid, and her moan of pleasure would definitely have embarrassed her if anyone else had heard.

"All right, I'll try."

She did her best to remove her boots, her hands too cold to grip well. The cold hit her skin and bit into her flesh so quickly that it frightened her. But then she pressed her feet against his legs. Even through his trews, she could feel his warmth. She closed her eyes and allowed him to do whatever he wished.

Anything for his heat.

He tugged her closer, slipped his legs to either side of her feet, tucking the rest of her flush against him. Then he rested his head above hers. They were close enough together that she could pillow her head on his folded plaid. He adjusted the other two plaids to cover them both.

She stared straight at his chest and blast it all, but she could see the muscles there. She did the only thing she could. She rested her head against his chest, the beating of his heart calming her.

Reveling in his heat, she smiled, soaking up all he had to give, but then she felt a strange pressure against her belly.

A large, hard, hot projection poked her, seeming to grow longer moment by moment.

"Alaric?"

"Sorry, lass. 'Tis natural. I wish to stop it, but I cannae. I'll still behave myself. Ye have my word of honor."

She leaned her head back to look at him, and she judged his expression to be quite sincere.

Oh, she knew what it was. Her cousins and the kitchen lasses had educated her verra well over the years.

The pole on the hill.

The rod of the mountain peak.

The throbbing member.

The stiff one.

The hard meat of his manhood.

And last but not least, the simplest but clearest name—the hot one.

Isla had said she wished to salute Grif's full mast one day, and the others had giggled hysterically.

Now she truly understood.

Curiosity got the best of her. "Can I touch it?"

"I wouldnae suggest…och…too late."

She wrapped her hand around his manhood, the heat warming her hand so much that she wished to wrap her foot around it but decided that would not be the best idea.

The moan of pleasure from Alaric at just her touch shocked her. She squeezed it just a bit and he moaned again, stilling her hand with his.

"Please dinnae," he ground out, sweat beading on his forehead unlike she'd ever seen before.

"Does it hurt ye?"

"Nay, it doesnae, but 'twill be a different kind of torture if ye dinnae take yer hand away. Please, lass."

"Ye are sweating in this cold?"

"Aye." The one word came out quiet and strangled, as if he choked on it.

The change in him gave her new insight into the relationship between a man and a woman.

The twitch in his jaw, the way his eyes closed slowly with his moan of pleasure gave her a sudden sense of power.

Were all men like this?

His hand reached over and caressed her breast through her tunic. "Will this warm ye at all, lass? It works for me, it must work for ye too."

She forced the shock back inside—her curiosity was stronger. No one would ever learn the truth of their encounter. This was the safest chance she'd ever have to experiment with sex.

It was time she learned. She took his hand and guided it underneath her tunic. She wished to see exactly how his hand felt on her breast, but she also wanted the warmth of his skin. His thumb brushed the tip of her nipple and a spark shot through her straight to her lady parts.

More curious than ever, she moved closer to him. She took his other hand and moved it under her tunic. Since she had two breasts, she saw no reason for him not to caress them both.

And it worked. She was warming up, partly from Alaric but also from the reaction her body was having to the physical stimulation. She knew how the act took place, and now that she held him in her hand, she envisioned how that heat would feel between her legs, so she moved him there, right where she wanted him. The heat traveled through her leggings, which surprised her. "Am I hurting ye? Should I stop?"

Alaric tipped his head down and closed his eyes, shaking his head. She squeezed her legs together against him just a wee bit and he moaned again, squeezing her nipples.

"Ye better stop, lass, if ye don't want to do something ye might regret."

Her curiosity was getting the better of her. If she could warm up from completing the act, then why not? She had no intention of marrying, so there was no reason to keep her virginity intact. Why not use it to suit her needs instead of some man's?

The truth came to her then, but she tried her best to deny it.

She wanted that man to be Alaric. She didn't understand why, but she trusted him. He was handsome, kind, and she actually had feelings for him. This was a far better situation than some random lad in the stables. And since there would never be a wedding, this was the best way for her to learn all about the act.

"I think I would like this inside me." There was something powerful going on inside her own body, and she wished to see exactly what it was. If she ever had to explain to anyone why she did it, the simple answer was to stay alive. She was about to freeze to death, and if she could find a way to fit this hot rod in her hand inside her, she would finally be warm. Surely anyone who'd spent a night in the cold would understand her meaning. They would surely believe her, would they not?

Then the oddest thing happened. Alaric squeezed her nipples again, and she shivered—but not from the cold. A need developed inside her that she wished to satisfy. Now she had to figure out exactly how to go about it. She reached for his member again and wrapped her hand around him.

Alaric groaned, a sound that was both pain and pleasure. Then he pulled her hand away from him. "Stop."

She did, watching his face. The poor man seemed to be in pain.

"Alaric, I am freezing cold. I need yer heat and that…thing of yers seems the best way to warm up. Please put it inside me."

"Nay, I canno' do this just to warm ye. 'Tis a foolish thing to say."

Annoyed that he didn't fall for her reasoning, she tried another tactic, one that was a wee bit closer to the truth. Her lady parts seemed to have a mind of their own and wanted that thing inside her. How she knew that, she wasn't quite sure, but she did.

He pulled himself away from her, and she began to shiver again. "Nay, please. I need ye, Alaric. I like the way ye are making me feel." That was the simple truth.

"Nay. I'll no' be bedding ye unless ye promise to marry me. My sire would kill me if I took yer maidenhead and we werenae married or at least promised to each other."

"I dinnae care anything about my maidenhead. I dinnae need it. I'm never marrying, so I choose to give it to ye. Please."

"Never marry? Why would ye say so?"

"Because I dinnae need a man for anything.

I'll be fine by myself. I have a clan, a family. I'll have nieces and nephews, so I'll be fine without a husband. So I dinnae need my maidenhead. In fact, I'm sick of it. I wish to rid myself of it." With that, just to make sure he understood her, she reached for his manhood and wrapped her hand around it again. "It shrank."

"No' for long!" He let out a large growl when she squeezed it again.

Sure enough, it grew in her hand like some magical staff. She was quite enjoying this discovery. It was hot and smooth and so comforting that she slid her leggings down and squeezed it between her legs. "That feels so much better."

It was as if her lady parts were talking now.

"Nay!" He pushed her away, and her shivers shook her body. But it wasn't just from the cold. It was from something else, and she had to convince him to finish this.

"Alaric, I need ye. I'm no' worried about marrying ye because I'll no' survive the cold."

He stared at her. "Promise me ye'll marry me if we both survive this night and our patrol. Or at least handfast with me. Though I think this night with ye is more likely to kill me than any battle with the English."

"Fine. I'll handfast with ye. That way I can end it in a year. But please. I desperately want ye now."

CHAPTER TWELVE

A LARIC GROANED AND tugged her close to him, his mouth finding hers. He had to do something to stop her trembling and shivering and chattering teeth. He managed to slip out of his trews while he kissed her.

She pushed her leggings down and spread her legs, then taking him firmly in her hand and guiding him between her legs. She wanted him, and that drove his own need for her to a height he'd never experienced before.

She whimpered when he rolled her onto her back and moved between her legs, angling himself at her entrance, doing his best to tease her. She wriggled against him, whispering against his ear.

"Aye, more, Alaric. I feel yer heat. More, pleeeease."

His hands found her breasts again under her tunic, and he teased her nipple, pleased to feel her arching against him. Her nipples were so cold that they were already peaked. But when she squirmed beneath him, begging him for more, angling his manhood exactly where she wanted him, he knew she was coming undone.

She was driving their coupling more than he would have guessed. She writhed against him until he found himself fitting inside her entrance. Her slickness surprised him, and it drove him forward just a bit. He should move slowly, gently, if he were taking her maidenhead.

But her words drove him to finish the deed. "Alaric, ye are so hot and warming me everywhere. This feels so wonderful, I need ye more. Please come into me. More, please."

She rambled on in her need, begging him as she spread her legs wider. Any hesitancy he might have still felt disappeared. He pushed inside.

"Ow!" she shouted, pinching his shoulder.

"One moment. Give it a moment, lass. It will go away, I promise."

And sooner than he expected, she was moving against him, controlling their rhythm and positions so he was pulsing against her just right. They moved against each other in that wonderful dance that only happened between lovers. This was the magic of melding well with someone, of fitting together the way nature intended. He made himself go slowly until she punched him.

"Faster, damn ye!"

He obeyed, speeding up and going deeper inside her with each push. He could feel her contractions until she finally convulsed against him with a scream, and he finished with a roar.

He rolled onto his back, taking her with him until she was on top of him. He covered her with his plaid and kept his arms wrapped around her, panting in the aftermath of pleasure unlike any he'd ever had before. She collapsed against him, her breathing as fast as his own.

"Ye found yer pleasure, Eli?"

"I sure as hell did. I had no idea it could be so pleasing." She laughed, her cheek resting against his chest. "Your heart is beating so fast."

"Fast and happy," he murmured, kissing her forehead.

He rubbed circles on her back, then rolled onto his side, still cocooning her within his arms.

She was sound asleep. And the truth of it all hit him.

What the hell had they just done?

The next morning, Eli awakened a bit sore in various spots, including one she hadn't realized *could* be sore, but that didn't concern her. In fact, she was quite pleased with herself for her boldness with Alaric. His arms were still wrapped around her but she forced herself to push away a wee bit, just to check to see if he was still asleep.

He wasn't, instead looking at her with a sly grin. She gave him the same back. "Pleased with yerself, Grant?" she asked.

"Aye. And by the expression on yer face, Lady Ramsay, I'd say ye are just as pleased with yerself as I am."

"I cannae deny it. It was a most enjoyable night. Now the question is, can we find our way back to the path and the rest of the patrol?"

He gave her a quick kiss on the lips. The action confused her, but it also pleased her. After unraveling their intertwined limbs, he stood and then helped her to her feet. The cold hit her like a blast and she shivered, realizing how fortunate she was to have slept in his arms. She headed toward the mouth of the cave but he shouted, scaring the wits from her.

"What?"

"Lass, ye know no' who will be out there. Put yer leggings on."

She looked down at her bare legs and chuckled. "I suppose ye are correct, even though I dinnae need them for my first task."

"But Maitland could be looking for us. Have ye no dignity?"

She had to ponder that for a moment because she was unsure of her answer. It wouldn't have bothered her to walk out and take care of her needs before donning her leggings, but she supposed it made good sense to put them on. After all, she wouldn't like to be kidnapped half naked in just a tunic. And she did need her boots.

"Probably ye are right. I'll put them on." She chuckled as she balanced on one foot to put her clothing on, then her boots. "Have we any food left?"

"I only have a couple of oatcakes. Ye?"

"None," she said as they headed out of the cave.

They both took care of their needs and met near their horses.

"What say ye, lass? Try to find the others or head home?"

Eli took a bit of an oatcake and looked around as she chewed. "The mist is gone, so we should try to find our way back to the path. The place we'd said we would meet." Then she gave him a saucy look. "Or we could do what we did last night. One more time?"

He stared at her wide-eyed. "Are ye no' sore?"

She shrugged. "Mayhap a wee bit. But I'm sure it will go away quickly."

Alaric glanced over his shoulder.

"What?"

"Naught." He kissed her on the lips too quickly for her to react. "I think we should move on. Try to find the group."

"One more time? I like that there is no one to worry about. No one here to watch us."

He whipped his head around to look behind him.

"What? Why do ye keep looking over yer shoulder? No one is there."

"Ye cannae see him? Because I surely can." His face went pale with fright. She'd never seen him look so.

"Who?" She moved him off to the side and stared where he was looking. "There is no one there."

"Aye, there is." He pointed at nothing Eli could see but trees and undergrowth.

"Where?"

"Right there. My grandsire Alex."

Eli stared at him. "Alaric, yer grandfather passed away last Yule."

"I know. But that cannae stop him from watching us. Probably makes it easier. He saw us last night. We arenae married, so now he's hounding me."

The fear in his face was surely real. And she didn't know how to tell him that the act of handfasting meant naught to her. But if it would help him ignore the ghost of his grandsire, she would do it.

She knew exactly how ornery grandparents could be.

"Alaric, he cannae be here. He's dead!"

"His spirit is no' dead, 'tis quite alive and glaring at me. And if my grandmama shows up, we'll be finding a kirk. But until then, we have to handfast. Your choice, lass—marry in the first kirk we come to or handfast now."

"We did handfast."

"No' officially." The sweat broke out across his forehead again. "Please? He'll no' leave me be until we do. I swear that every time I look over my shoulder, he will be there. Please, Eli."

"Fine. He doesn't spook me, but if he's bothering ye, then we can handfast. But I thought we already did."

"Nay, we only spoke of it." He held his hand out and said, "Give me yer hand."

She gave him a skeptical look.

"I'm doing it, Grandpapa!" He looked behind him again. "Eli, would ye like to have yer grandsire looking over yer shoulder all the time? Alexander Grant would be ten times worse. I have to get rid of him. Hellfire. He heard that." He turned all the way around and held out his hands placatingly. "I do love ye, Grandpapa, just no' so much when yer ghost hovers and glares like that. I'll fix it!"

Eli put her hand over her mouth to hide her grin. He truly believed his grandfather was watching them and, apparently, sending a very clear message.

Alaric turned back to her. "Ye think 'tis amusing, but ye'll see someday when yer grandsire passes on and watches everything ye do."

Eli scowled, that thought too frightening. She shuddered at the thought. "Well, that would be disconcerting, I suppose."

"Take my hand, Eli," Alaric urged, his voice commanding now.

"Dinnae panic, Alaric. Logan Ramsay is already looking over my shoulder all the time, but I'll agree if 'twill please ye."

"Logan wasn't here to see us last night, was he? That would be the difference."

She couldn't argue that and stifled a second shudder. "Ye make a fair point." She held out her hand, and he took it, tossing the end of his plaid over their intertwined fingers. Then he repeated some Gaelic phrases and said, "I agree to handfast to ye, Eli Ramsay, for a year and a day. Do ye agree?"

"Aye. Sure."

He leaned over and kissed her, then pulled the plaid back, dropping her hand.

"Is he gone?"

He looked back and then smiled. "Aye, he's gone."

Crushing pain slammed into Eli's shoulder. "Ach!" She bent double, hand to the invisible wound.

"Eli! What's wrong?" Alaric gripped her arms and held her.

"My shoulder hurts, like someone put an arrow in it."

As if that wasn't enough, her knee began to ache, just as it had when her grandmother had fallen in the great hall. She bent over to massage it.

"Does yer knee hurt too?" Alaric asked. He looked around, as if he might spot the archer shooting phantom arrows.

"Aye. They both hurt. Help me get on my horse. We need to find the others. I think something has happened."

He helped her mount, then climbed into his own saddle and they headed back the direction they had come from the night before. It didn't take them long to find their way to the true path now that the mist was gone.

When they could ride abreast again, Alaric looked at her with concern in his eyes.

"What is going on, Eli? I cannae see any blood. Are ye injured?"

"Nay. I have no idea what happened. I'm not truly hurt. Let's hurry, though."

She motioned for him to move along, and he didn't ask again. Which was good. She'd nearly told him the truth, that she would sometimes feel other people's pain, especially if they were injured. Her grandmother's knee was worse than it had been when she'd left Ramsay land. Of that she was certain. But the shoulder pain concerned her.

Someone she knew had taken a shoulder injury. But who?

CHAPTER THIRTEEN

THEY MADE IT back to where their group had split up the previous day, though all three paths were empty.

"Which way do ye wish to travel?" Alaric asked. Eli grimaced, and she rubbed her knee again. "How is yer pain? Can ye ride, lass?"

"Better. Both spots ache, but the pain has eased. And as much as I have enjoyed our time together, I think I can confidently say that neither one of us is an expert at wayfinding, and I dread the thought of searching for the others blindly. We dinnae know the area, and we have no idea where they ended up. What if they got lost in the mist or have already turned back? We have no idea."

Alaric couldn't disagree with her. "I suppose we should head back to Ramsay land. We've only been gone a day, but I'm anxious to see if there is any word on my brother's recovery. 'Tis the safest place to rendezvous."

"Then we head north to Ramsay land. At least we know where we're going when we go in that direction."

"And since we are alone, I hope ye will share something with me."

She turned her horse to head north and rode abreast of him. "What can I tell ye?"

"Why do ye think yer grandsire dislikes ye? I dinnae think of Logan that way at all. He adores his family, his clan, and most of all his grandbairns. I think ye have it all wrong."

"Because whenever we were training in archery, he made me practice more than the others. I'm the weakest archer, and he couldn't accept that I'd never be as good as the other lasses. He was constantly pushing me to be better."

"All parents and grandparents do that, do they no'?"

"I suppose when we were young, it was all the same, but as we got older, he began to treat me differently. One time, I was shooting and I hit a rabbit by mistake. I ran to it and my grandsire went wild, yelling for me to stop, to go home, to get away from the poor creature. It was so bad, I embarrassed him and he sent me away. The others—my sister and cousins—all laughed at me."

Alaric couldn't help it—he moved his horse closer to her. "Poor wee Eli. I think he was trying to help ye, but the others shouldn't have laughed. Ye are the youngest, are ye no'?"

"One of the youngest. Lainey is younger by a long shot, but I was younger than the group being trained—Cadyn, Ceit, Ysenda, Reyna, Isla. And then there was me. And dinnae feel sorry for me, ye churlish bastard."

"We made love and handfasted and ye still curse at me?" What was it with this lass and the cursing? He had to admit that it was fun teasing her. It was easy to get a foul word from her if he tried.

"All right, I'll try to stop. But I make no promises and I do sincerely hope ye find yer brother is better. I know how it feels to worry and not be able to help. I felt the same when Ysenda broke her leg."

They topped a rise and caught sight of four riders ahead of them. Eli pointed. "Is that no' them?"

"I think it is." He let out a loud whistle, and one rider turned around. It was Tevis.

Eli yelled, "Wait! We'll join ye!"

Alaric sighed in relief, glad to see their group. They could have made it home, but with both of their senses of direction being poor, there were no promises. He would make sure they didn't travel alone again if they were heading into a new area.

"What happened to ye?" Dyna asked as soon as they were within earshot.

Eli replied quickly. "We found a cave to wait out the downpour and then when we tried to leave, the damn mist was everywhere. We couldn't retrace our steps when we couldn't see any landmarks."

"We waited for ye but when ye didn't come, we decided to ride back north. I'm glad ye are well."

"Does anyone have a shoulder injury?" Eli asked, looking from one to the next. Wenna turned sideways to show the blood on her tunic. "Wenna! What happened?"

Wenna rolled her eyes. "An attack by the English, but in the mist, we never saw them coming."

"We were badly outnumbered," Maitland explained. "Nearly a score to our four. We needed ye, surely, but I still would not have taken on a score. Dyna hit her marks as usual, and Wenna hit two herself before she was wounded. We put up enough of a fuss that even though we were already running, they were pulling back. I was pleased they didnae decide to pursue us."

"Why would they attack ye for just being on the road?" Alaric asked. What would the English want with four Scottish travelers? "If ye had been carrying provisions, I might understand. But why would they bother with the four of ye? They have naught to gain from ye."

"Bragging, I suppose. Possibly our horses or just the killing of four Scots."

"They looked hungry in more than the usual way," Tevis added. "They probably had ideas for the two women. If they were from Edinburgh, they haven't had women in Berwick for quite some time. I didnae like the way they looked at Dyna and Wenna."

Maitland nodded. "I thought the same. Now we are headed to Ramsay land to get Wenna's wound tended, then we shall return. I'll no' chase that group down unless we have at least eight and have the high ground. I didnae like the numbers we just encountered. We need to recruit before we can join with Sir James."

"If ye arenae in a hurry, I can return to Grant land and see if I can recruit anyone," Alaric said. "I'd like to check on my brother, if ye dinnae mind. One night and I'll head back."

"Suits me fine," Maitland said. "We'll return to Ramsay land together, then send Dyna with ye and we'll await yer return."

Dyna turned to assess Eli and Alaric, her gaze narrowing at both of them. "Anything happen between ye two? Ye seem on edge."

Eli narrowed her eyes at Alaric in apparent warning, so he said nothing, waiting for her to answer.

"It's just that I'm sure Grandmama's knee is worse. Sometimes I can feel it, just like my shoulder began to ache this morn. I want to see what's happening at home. And sleeping in a cold, damp cave is no' very restful."

Alaric nodded in agreement, unsure of what to add.

Maitland smirked, and Dyna arched a brow at both of them.

Eli, in her finest scornful tone, drawled, "And if ye think we are anything like Brin and Ceit, ye can be sure we werenae. He's lucky he's still alive, the churlish bastard, with all the teasing and taunting he threw my way. I told him if we didnae find ye quickly, he would surely regret it."

Alaric shrugged. "I was worried about my brother, and she's worried about her grandmother.

"Thank the Lord we're going our separate ways soon."

And he had to wonder if she meant it.

CHAPTER FOURTEEN

ELI HAD TO admit that she didn't really want Alaric to leave. She'd gotten used to him being around, but she also respected his need to check on his brother. She could easily recall how unsettled she'd been when she found out Ysenda had gone over the ravine in an avalanche. Only actually seeing her sister had calmed her worries.

She only had one sister, after all. She loved her brother, of course, but sisters were different. Alaric had four siblings—Els, Jowell, Merelda, and Maryell. And he had many more cousins than she did.

They stopped at the edge of Ramsay land for a short break, and the other members of their group tended to their needs and stretched their legs. Eli needed to get a solemn promise from Alaric before they rode any farther. She made sure they were out of earshot before speaking.

"Promise ye will tell no one."

"What?"

Her voice dropped to a whisper. "Tell no one that we handfasted. I dinnae want anyone to know."

"Why no'? I was going to tell my brother if he is awake. Do I embarrass ye?"

"Nay," she said, not wishing to insult Alaric. If she were going to handfast with anyone, she would choose him over any other, she realized with a jolt. "I just dinnae wish to explain it yet. 'Tis more important to get back on this patrol and take care of the English from Berwick Castle. Once this is over, we'll tell people. But for now. Do. Not. Tell." She glared at him, trying to convince him with her eyes alone.

"Fine, lass. 'Tis no' a concern for me yet. We have more important things to do. I'll agree it can wait a moon. But after that, I'm telling. Ye never know what could happen." Then he glanced at her belly.

Blast it all, she hadn't given that a thought. Carrying a bairn? She guessed it was time to start praying again. She wasn't the best at it, but God seemed to understand her, as far as she could tell. Eli had always believed God to be a female, so of course She would understand a woman's concerns. Her grandmother had suggested it once to upset a bunch of men, and she liked the idea. Anyway, she'd say her prayers, and God would make sure she wasnae carrying.

"Godspeed with ye, and I pray yer brother has healed."

"I wish the same for ye and yer grandmother." He leaned forward to give her a peck on her cheek, but she leaned back, giving him a glare.

He laughed and winked at her.

The group split, Alaric and Dyna riding toward

Grant Castle, while the remaining four headed to Ramsay land. Eli sank into her thoughts as she rode. The first thing she would do once she arrived would be to check on her grandmother. The ache in her shoulder had calmed, but the ache in her knee was the same.

"I dinnae know who he is after, but here comes Uncle Logan," Maitland said.

Eli let out a groan, and she didn't attempt to squelch it one bit. "Bloody hell."

Maitland grinned at her. "New curse word? Ye sound like Dyna now."

"I like 'bloody hell.' Says exactly how I feel."

"And ye are sure he is after ye?"

This time, Wenna, Tevis, and Maitland all gave her wide grins. Wenna whispered, "I hope ye are right. I dinnae need to be stopped. I'm going to visit Aunt Brenna."

"As ye should." Eli couldn't disagree with her, though she was looking for anyone to distract her grandfather. "Grandsire is always roaming about Ramsay land. 'Tis the only way he'd catch all the messengers. He stays up on all the happenings in the land that way. He's permanently on patrol my father says." She hoped that's all his purpose was, but she could see he directed his gaze straight at her. "Blast it all to hell and back," she muttered.

Maitland glanced at her with a grin. "Feeling his gaze, are ye?"

"Aye," she mumbled. "Tevis, need ye to speak with my grandsire?"

"No' me, lass. I'm going with Wenna. She needs help dismounting." His smile grew, and Eli thought Wenna's hope that Tevis liked her was probably coming true.

Her grandsire came closer and his voice rang out loud and clear. "Eli! A word with ye in private, if ye please. Maitland, why have ye returned so early?" He stopped in the middle of the path, his horse blocking their way.

"We were attacked by a large group of English soldiers. We got our hits in, but we were hit too. Wenna needs Aunt Brenna. Will ye let us pass, Uncle Logan?"

Her grandfather moved off the path.

"I'll see her to Aunt Brenna's," Tevis said.

The two left, and her grandfather watched Eli for a moment before speaking to Maitland again. "English came at ye from where?"

"I dinnae know. They had nearly a score, and only four of us at the time. Eli and Alaric lost their path in the storm and fog and didn't rejoin us until later in the day."

Eli nearly groaned but managed to keep her displeasure about the secret reveal to herself. Her grandfather didn't miss it, shooting her another look. "Eli and Alaric, eh?" He grunted. "And where is Alaric now? And Dyna? Not hurt?"

"Nay. They took the road to Grant land to check on Els. We need to recruit a few more fighters, so they'll see who is available, then meet up here in two days. I willnae go south unless I have six traveling, but more would be better based on what we saw out there."

"Sounds like a wise precaution."

"Aye. 'Twill only be more English farther

south," Maitland said. "I'm going to ride on, since ye wish to speak to Eli. I hope there's food at the castle."

Her grandfather laughed. "Aye, plenty. Eli and I will follow ye."

Maitland moved ahead, casting her a pitying glance, but she could handle her grandfather. "What has ye bothered, Grandda?"

"No' bothered, just wondering if ye arranged things with Alaric. Did ye talk to him about the alliance?"

She stopped her horse with a jerk on the reins. "Nay! And stop asking me. What is yer obsession with Alaric? Can I no' decide who I marry? And why do ye always pick on me?"

"I dinnae always pick on ye. Ye are daft, lass." He waved his hand in dismissal at her.

That only aggravated her more. "Ye do."

"Never have. I know no' what ye are speaking of. Tell me what ye mean."

"Ye dinnae recall the day ye yelled at me when I was shooting at the range and hit a rabbit? And I always had to shoot more than the others. They would leave, and ye'd make me shoot ten more. Why is that?"

Grandsire looked more riled than she expected. "Aye, I told ye to stop because ye were busy staring at the rabbit. And then ye tried to fix it somehow. The animal was already dead. Ye killed it. There was no room for guilt. I was trying to toughen ye up, lass. Who the hell looks at dead animals besides Brenna? And ye had to shoot more because ye were younger. When the others were first learning, they shot more, too. And their teasing would break yer concentration, so I kept ye after so ye could practice alone. Is this really why ye are so riled up, Elisant Ramsay? Seems like there's something else worrying at ye, girl." His gray hair blew in the wind, making him look older than he was, but the crafty eyes never aged.

She could never lie to him and get away with it, so she didn't try. She just didn't tell him all. "Naught is wrong. But I'm worried about Grandmama. How is her knee?"

Her grandfather cursed under his breath and turned his horse back toward home. "Her knee is worse. Brenna is doing her best with all her ointments and potions, but they arenae working yet. She always says to give it time. Well, Gwynie and I dinnae have much time anymore."

"Sometimes it does take time. Especially when the leakage turns green. Ye know it works slow. Even Aunt Jennie says so." Eli had watched many of the healers over the years, asking questions and helping whenever possible. She found the art of healing very interesting.

"I'll be going for Aunt Jennie soon. Ye can mark my words. But go visit with yer grandmama. She's no' happy when it hurts too much to walk outside. She's stuck in our bedchamber."

"I'll do that." The castle came into sight, Maitland almost to the gates. Eli sighed. "I'm sorry I yelled, Grandda. I love ye."

"I love ye too, Eli. Sometimes I may sound daft, but I have my reasons. Go find something to eat. I'll chat with ye later." They reached

Aunt Bethia's house, and he waved her on. "I'm stopping to check on Donnan and Thea."

Eli was glad to have a few moments to herself. At least she had a plan now. Her biggest concern was her grandmother, but her belly was telling her she needed to feed it first. She left her horse at the stable with a lad, grabbed her saddle bag, then made her way inside. She rummaged through the bag quickly. Everything inside was drenched or dirty or both.

She had to pack better for the next trip.

After filling her belly and leaving her belongings in her chamber, she headed over to her grandmother's room, not surprised to find her grandfather had returned to his beloved wife's side by the time she arrived. They lived on the ground floor of one of the towers now that Grandmama had trouble climbing stairs. They had a central chamber with a hearth to the outside, and two bedchambers opened off of that central room. Uncle Cailean and Aunt Sorcha slept upstairs, because Sorcha liked to keep an eye on her mother.

As soon as Eli stepped into the chamber, her grandsire came out to greet her and started on her all over again.

"So did ye handfast with Alaric or no'? Ye never answered me before."

"Why must ye keep pushing me to marry Alaric, Grandda? Ye havenae pushed anyone else. They've all found their own."

He scowled and grumbled but said nothing.

Grandmama yelled from the next chamber. "Because I pushed him to do it."

Had she heard correctly? Her grandmother wanted her to marry Alaric? She didn't believe it. "She's covering for yer stubbornness, Grandda."

The old man looked aghast. "*My* stubbornness?"

"Eli, please join me. Logan, go away."

"Gladly, Gwynie. I'm going to the stables."

Eli heard the door slam as she entered her grandmother's chamber.

Her larger-than-life grandmother sat in the far corner, her leg propped on a stool, her knee still visibly swollen. Eli couldn't help but admire her because she'd earned herself a reputation over the years as a formidable archer. And it was such a fierce reputation that it put the fear of God into any man whenever they discovered she was nearby. Every time Eli had heard the story about Grandmama pinning a man to a tree by his bollocks for messing with her granddaughters, she had to smile. Unfortunately, her eyes had failed her long before her skill with a bow. But she'd dedicated herself to teaching others, especially any lasses in the clan.

"Yer knee looks terrible. Is it no' any better?"

"Would I be here if I could go elsewhere? Ye know I hate sitting inside."

She did know that. Her grandmother was still slender from keeping active. She kept her hair plaited, the salt and pepper strands beautiful in Eli's eyes.

"Was it truly yer idea for me to marry Alaric, Grandmama? Why?"

Her grandmother let out a huge sigh and patted the arm of the chair next to her. "I didnae wish for ye to know so I told Logan my idea. Sit down, Eli. We need to talk."

"Nay. I dinnae know if I can listen to this. I thought ye were my biggest supporter, no' the one trying to control me." Close to yelling at her beloved grandmother, she caught the distressed look on the woman's face and pulled in her temper.

"Sit down and listen, please."

She did as her grandmother instructed, but she wasn't clear minded enough to listen to her.

"And take that look off yer face. Look, I know ye as well as yer own mother does. And it was I, not Logan, who wished for ye to marry Alaric. I'll admit it."

"Why? I dinnae understand this at all. I thought ye loved me."

"I do. Before I die, I wish I could see all my grandbairns settled, but ye most of all."

Eli shook her head in denial and opened her mouth to speak, but her grandmother wagged her finger at her.

"Hush, lass. Allow me to speak my mind while I still have it."

She owed her that much, so nodded and leaned back in her chair to listen.

"I pushed ye harder than the others. 'Tis true. I'll no' deny it, but I had my reasons. Ye have the quickest mind of any of my granddaughters. I know ye'll no' believe it, but ye do. I can teach anyone to shoot an arrow at a target, but a quick mind that is open to all possibilities, that questions things, that can see other points of view and see the whole picture? I cannae teach that. Ye are born with that sense and intelligence. Ye have it."

Eli was stunned. She'd always thought the others were all quicker-minded than she was. She resisted the urge to express her disbelief and let her grandmother go on.

"When ye were young, I watched ye. Oh, Reyna was a powerful archer, but ye were faster thinking than any of the others, and they saw it too. So they began to pick on ye and tease ye until ye began to give in to them and stopped arguing. Ye let them win at things they shouldn't have, but I didnae stop it. I figured ye would grow up and when ye were wise enough, ye would stand up to them and show them who was the wisest one. But instead, ye became angry and all knotted up inside. I still dinnae know why, but if ye would let go of yer anger, ye would be the quickest of all.

"And I believe in alliances. I spoke with Connor one day about all his nephews, and he said Alaric showed the most promise. He called him level-headed, witty, with a sense of humor that others didn't have. He claimed that Alaric had the best sense of being a leader, that he could size up a situation faster than anyone else. Make decisions quickly. Something Connor thinks he himself cannae do well enough yet."

She paused to rub her knee and Eli started to speak, but her grandmother held her hand up again. "I'm no' finished." She took a sip of ale and settled again.

"There is trouble coming for Scotland, and our two clans need to have the best guidance ever. I believed that ye and Alaric could be the alliance we need to show the other clans how united we are. Ye have the wisdom, the quick mind, and the courage to be a leader. And so does Alaric, and he has the even temper to steady yers and nudge ye out of the sulks. The two of ye would be a powerful couple. But ye have to stop fighting destiny, lass."

Eli frowned, not knowing what to say to her grandmother. The dear woman had given her too much to absorb and used words she'd never heard before. Intelligence, wisdom, courage. No one had ever used those words when they spoke of Elisant Ramsay.

"Ye and Alaric Grant belong together. I can see it. How long will it take ye to see it?"

She nearly cried but stopped the tears. After all, she hadn't cried in years, and she wasn't about to start now. "Ye've given me much to think on, Grandmama, but we have another patrol to run. I'll think on yer words and let ye know how I feel when I return. I hardly know him at this point." That was only a small lie. They'd ridden patrols together before, but not spoken much, except to snipe at each other. Before the night in the cave, she'd thought she'd hated Alaric. Now, she had to admit she liked his personality. But she would not admit—yet—that she'd given the man her maidenhead and that they'd handfasted.

She would not give her grandparents that satisfaction. Not yet. It would be akin to admitting she'd been wrong and saying she'd allow them to dictate her future. Nay—she would do this in her own way.

She chose Alaric, not her grandparents.

Her grandmother sighed again. "That will suit me fine, lass. Have a good patrol. Find the English bastards and take them out." Then she leaned her head back and closed her eyes.

Eli was totally lost now.

Even though she'd handfasted with Alaric, she hadn't intended it to be permanent. She had planned to back out of it long before the year and a day. If Alaric was upset, so be it. In fact, she'd planned to let him know right away that she hadn't meant what she said. But maybe that was not the best option. Because now it wouldn't just upset Alaric but also her grandmother.

And what if she were carrying Alaric's bairn?

CHAPTER FIFTEEN

A LARIC AND DYNA arrived on Grant land by the end of the day.

"Ye check on yer brother," Dyna said. "I'll find out from the others how he fares. Rest up, fill yer belly and yer saddlebag while I go search for anyone to recruit."

Alaric nodded, nearly afraid to take the necessary steps to the healing chamber where he'd last seen his brother.

Dyna somehow sensed his hesitation, because she gave him another push. "Bloody hell, just go in, Alaric. I'm going to the tower to look for Derric and my father. I'm sure ye'll find yer sire in the hall."

Dyna strode off, and Alaric took a deep breath and headed for the great hall. He was pleased to see his mother and father both there, bickering as usual. His sire still had a splint on his leg to keep him from moving it around. The man wouldn't tolerate that for long.

"How much longer, Gracie? Surely I'm healing faster than most," his father was saying, as if he'd heard Alaric's thoughts.

"Yer aunt said at least a moon, Jamie. Perhaps two. 'Tis a bad break, and it will take longer to heal."

"I'm no' staying in the hall for a moon. Never."

"And if ye break yer leg again and start all over because ye disobeyed orders?"

"Ye are surely the pessimist today, Gracie Grant."

His mother threw her arms in the air. "Jamie, I love ye much and ye know it. But every day ye tell me all the things ye willnae do. I am no' the expert. I willnae tell ye to do anything different than Aunt Jennie instructed. I trust her judgment. Do ye no'?"

His father grumbled something he couldn't hear, but then his mother noticed Alaric had arrived. "Alaric! I'm pleased to see ye. But why are ye home so soon? Are ye hale?"

He moved forward to give his mother a swift hug and clasped his sire's shoulder, his fear of jostling him too strong to move any closer. "I'm well, Mama. Wenna was injured in a skirmish, so we turned back so she might be tended. I see Da is still testing yer patience. Da, is yer pain any better?"

"Aye, as long as I dinnae move it, it willnae hurt me. But a moon no' moving is a long time. I dinnae know if I can do it."

"Didnae Ysenda have some contraption so she could eventually get around with some help? It was after a few weeks, I think. Can ye no' ride on a horse with it? Mayhap ye'll be able to use that soon. How is Els?"

"Yer brother is better," his mother said, the smile

on her face telling him that she was pleased with how things were progressing. "He's awakened. He isnae talking yet, but Aunt Jennie said that could take a while to return."

"What about the swelling? Is it down?"

"No' yet. It is much improved, though, so I'm hoping that when it goes completely away that mayhap his speech will return. Why do ye no' go visit with him?"

"Have ye anything I can eat to take with me?" He was suddenly starving. The few bites of oatcake he'd had early that morning had long since worn off.

"Aye, I see half a loaf of bread on the sideboard, and I think I see some cheese. I'll look for some meat for ye." She left at such a quick pace that Alaric suspected the poor woman was anxious to get away from his father.

His father sighed heavily once she left the great hall. "She tests my patience sometimes. And I'm no' a good patient."

"She has two of ye to worry about, no' just ye, Da. Ye know she has the biggest heart ever, and ye should know how sensitive she is."

"I know. And I know I'm a wee bit ornery, but I hate being so idle. I'll apologize to her. How long are ye home for?"

"Only one night, so I could see ye and Els and Dyna could find some more recruits to ride this patrol with us."

"She'll no' find many. Mayhap one or two. Go see yer brother. I know ye need to do that first."

His father waved him on, so he stepped to the

sideboard, grabbed the bread and cheese before heading to the healing chamber.

He put a bit of the cheese with the bread and took a bite. His stomach was doing summersaults just from the thought of his brother awake. Stopping outside the door to the healing chamber, Alaric finished chewing before he opened the door just enough to peek around it.

Els was propped up in the bigger bed, mounds of pillows behind him, and Joya sat in a chair feeding their wee bairn, Seamus. She covered herself quickly as he stepped inside, but it wouldn't have mattered. Feeding a babe was the most natural thing in the world, in his opinion. And he only had eyes for his brother anyway.

His brother's gaze caught his.

"Els? Ye are awake!"

He'd never seen a more beautiful sight. The sparkle was back in his brother's gaze. His golden locks were a wavy mess, but he nodded to Alaric, and nothing could have pleased him more.

Alaric set his food on a table and pulled a stool over next to the bed. "Ye are hale again?"

His brother smiled and nodded again but said nothing. Alaric looked to Joya who explained, "He's awake and able to understand ye, but he's no' talking yet. And he's moving his hands and feet, but he is no' strong enough yet to walk."

"But he's awake, and that's the important part."

His brother smiled and nodded.

Unable to stop himself, Alaric reached to the back of Els's head. The bump was still there— smaller by far, but still there. As if reading his mind, Joya said, "We're hoping that when it's gone down completely, his words will return."

Els nodded, slowly touching his head with his hand, an effort for sure.

"It still pains ye?"

Els nodded.

"Aunt Jennie left a potion to help with his headaches so he can sleep," Joya said.

He finally had the chance to apologize, so he decided to do it now while it was just the two of them and Joya. "Els, I just want to offer my apologies for telling ye to go down the hill. I shouldn't have said aught…"

Els shook his head and his eyes darted back and forth furiously.

"What is it? I'm sorry ye got hurt because of me."

Els shook his head again and a loud groan came out as if he were trying to speak. Alaric looked to Joya to see what she made of this change in demeanor. "Joya?"

"I think he's trying to tell ye no' to apologize. Is that right, Els?"

Els nodded.

"'Tis no' yer fault, Alaric. Ye didnae make the rain come. Ye didnae hold a knife to Els's back and force him down the hill."

Els nodded and tears trickled down his cheeks.

That was too much for Alaric. He got up and left.

Joya called out after him. "Alaric?"

"Sorry, Joya. I have to go. I'll be back later. I'm sorry I upset him." Then he spun around one more time to look at his brother, his arms up in a gesture of helplessness. "I'm so sorry, Els!"

He hated seeing anyone cry, but especially his beloved brother. Nothing had ever upset him more than the tears in his brother's eyes.

CHAPTER SIXTEEN

A LARIC WENT STRAIGHT through the hall to the main door, but it opened before he could grab the handle. Uncle Connor nearly knocked him down coming through.

"Good day, Uncle Connor. I was just heading out to the stables to look for Dyna."

"Dyna's busy. I'd like to talk with ye and Jamie first, if ye dinnae mind." Connor was the uncle who most resembled Alaric's grandfather, the renowned Alexander Grant. Tall, broad-shouldered, long dark hair that curled where it hit at his shoulders. He kept his muscles strong by working in the lists at least four times a sennight.

"Fine with me," he said, glancing over at his father to see if he was awake. Jamie waved at them, no doubt alert to all that happened in the hall.

"Connor, come on over," his father called. "No one but Gracie is around, and she just left to tend Els."

His father hadn't moved from the hearth and the stool for his leg. Alaric's grandfather had used that stool himself for many years.

A serving lass stepped out from the kitchen, but Connor waved her away. "Leave us for half the hour, please, Gillis." The lass nodded and returned to the kitchen.

"Ye see yer brother has improved, aye, Alaric?" Uncle Connor asked, taking the seat next to Jamie. Connor and Jamie had been co-lairds of the clan since their eldest brother Jake had passed on.

"Aye. I was pleased to see that sparkle in his eyes again, but he's not doing as well as I'd like. I hoped once he awakened, he'd be the same as he'd been before."

"We all hoped for that," Jamie said. "But think about how long it will take me to heal my leg. He hurt his brain. 'Tis how Gracie explained it to me. His brain swelled and it takes a while to return to the way it was. I hope not the two moons she says it will take my leg to fix, but at least he's awakened and understands us. Joya is happy with that small gift."

"I am too." Alaric leaned forward, settling his elbows on his knees and rubbing his hands together. If he could do anything to help his brother he would. Anything.

"Alaric," Connor started. "I know ye are going on patrol, but I offer this for yer consideration. I've already spoken with yer parents about this, but 'tis time to consider something."

"All right." Alaric straightened, getting the feeling this would be something important.

"Yer father is frustrated and knows it will take

time for him to heal. Aunt Jennie said the break was bad and his leg may not heal straight."

He looked to his father for his reaction. His sire nodded. "I'm no' going to rush myself back onto my feet, no matter how I grumble at Gracie. Much as I'd like to get going, Aunt Jennie made it clear that if I rush it, I could ruin my chances of a sound heal. I dinnae know exactly what it means, but I've seen others who dinnae get expert care after a break, and they end up with a crooked limb and cannae fight or sometimes even walk well. I dinnae want that. Some end up crippled for life."

"Aye, Da, I'm glad to hear ye plan to do what Aunt Jennie tells ye. And Mama. Look how well Ysenda has healed because she did exactly as Aunt Jennie and Aunt Brenna told her."

Jamie snorted. "I'm pleased ye approve, son. Go on, Connor."

Uncle Connor nodded, then took a deep breath. "We think that based on yer sire's and brother's conditions that ye should consider becoming co-laird with me instead of yer sire."

Both men turned their attention to Alaric, who could not have been more surprised. "Me?"

They nodded, giving him the time to think on his uncle's words. For that, he was grateful. He'd never considered this turn of events in his life. He'd known all along, as everyone else in the clan knew, that the lairdship passes on to the eldest child, usually the son, but on occasion a daughter. Kyla and Elizabeth both refused when Jake passed on, so that left it to Els or Alasdair in the future.

Uncle Connor went on. "I still have many years left in me, but when my time to step down comes, I hope Dyna will take my place, but if she refuses, we'll ask Alasdair. So there are other possibilities, but yer father would like ye to step up. 'Tis yer time, Alaric." Uncle Connor got up and made himself a cup of mead.

"But I know naught of being laird. I've never paid much attention to what ye do, Da." Alaric ran his hand through his hair, not sure he liked the way this conversation had turned.

"But I am here to guide ye, as is Connor. The two of us will lead ye, but I dinnae think ye'll need much guidance. After seeing how well ye reacted to the accident on the hill, I'm convinced ye are a natural to lead. Even more so than yer brother, in fact."

"When ye fell? What did I do?" Alaric couldn't be more dumbfounded by that comment.

Uncle Connor clapped Alaric on the shoulder. "By the time I arrived, ye had already taken care of nearly everything. The cart was on its way, ye had taken care of the seed, which will keep yer clanmates from starving this year. Ye were calm and knew exactly how to give directions. Ye handled it perfectly, Alaric. I was quite proud of ye."

His father nodded and said, "As we all were. I was shocked that anyone had the foresight to send the seed on. Ye saved us, Alaric. Ye took care of what I needed by ordering the cart, and ye had yer brother loaded on a horse and back to the keep in no time. Even with all that, ye remembered the seed. Only certain people can stay calm during catastrophes and see what matters most. Ye did. And I believe ye were the only one. By the time I thought of it, most of the seed would have been ruined."

"Nay, Da. If I hadn't made the wrong decision in the first place, ye and Els would both still be hale."

"And the seed would have been soaked through. Ye made the *right* decision, Alaric." His father turned to Uncle Connor. "I told ye this would shock him. Allow him to think on it."

"Aye," Uncle Connor said, standing up and clasping his shoulder again. "Go on this patrol and give us yer answer when ye return. In the meantime, there are others hoping ye'll train with them in the lists. And at least one person wants to spar with ye. Are ye ready?"

"I'll be glad to spar on the morrow. 'Twas a long day. I'm ready for some sleep." He'd gotten little rest the night before with Eli lying in his arms, but he'd not admit he was exhausted. He still had one more day before he and Dyna would head back. Alaric stood quickly, perhaps too quickly. Nothing sounded better to him than going out of the keep, away from his father, his brother, and all the questions in his mind. But not yet.

He felt best when he sparred, and he needed practice. But it would have to wait another day. As long as it was with anyone other than Alasdair.

"I'll be ready at first light. Are ye going that way?"

"Aye. I'd love to watch ye spar then. They'll

wait for ye until the morrow. And I think I know who is first in line."

Alaric held his breath.

"Alasdair cannae wait to spar with ye."

Shite. He was hoping to escape from challenging Alasdair.

"I'll need to warm up with someone else before I face Alasdair. Let him know that, Uncle. I'll be there on the morrow." His cousin was known as being one of the finest swordsmen in the clan. And he could not escape the unspoken tension he felt between himself and Alasdair. But one thing was certain.

He did not wish to spar with Alasdair.

CHAPTER SEVENTEEN

ELI WOKE UP the next morn with one problem cleared up. She was not carrying Alaric's bairn. The blood between her legs told her so.

She said a silent prayer of gratitude as she dressed for the day.

When she arrived at the great hall to break her fast, she was surprised to see Ysenda chatting with Maitland. Her sister waved her over so she joined the two. "Ysenda, ye are going with us?"

"Hell, nay. Never again. I did my duty, and I'm done. Besides, I truly think I am carrying."

"Well I'm glad I'm no'!" Realizing what she'd just said, her gaze darted to Ysenda's and Maitland's to see if they'd caught the true meaning of her words.

They had.

Ysenda grinned, and Maitland arched a brow at her.

"Do not ask. I was just reacting to my sister's comment. She might be, and I'm no'. And I had no reason to think I was. Enough said about that. Bloody hell."

"So do ye like Alaric?" her sister asked, still wearing a wide grin.

"Nay, and I wish people would all stop asking me that question. Why do they no' ask about Tevis and Wenna? They have their heads together giggling whenever I see them."

Maitland patted her arm. "Calm yerself, lass. We are teasing ye. Tevis and Wenna have admitted interest in each other, so no one asks. And they love to be alone. They do not protest when anyone brings it up. With ye and Alaric, 'tis simply conjecture, and yer temper about it makes it fun to poke. Ye are the only two on patrol who havenae found yer match."

"Have ye found anyone else to join us?" Eli changed the subject.

"Not for certes. Thea and Willum are considering joining us. They said they would let me know for sure before we leave on the morrow. I'm hoping Dyna recruits someone, but no one here is ready. And there really isn't anyone else to ask."

"Truly, there are others," Eli explained. Her brother for one, thought she already knew that her parents would not allow two of their children to be on the same patrol.

"There are, but many have no skills when it comes to a skirmish. They are of no use to us if they cannae strike down the enemy. Surely ye can see that."

She nodded. That point she couldn't argue. "I hope Thea and Willum come."

"I do too."

Eli's grandsire came into the hall, slamming the door as usual. "Menzie, chat with me outside, if ye please."

Maitland gave a quick nod to Ysenda and Eli, then left with Grandda.

"What do ye suppose that is about?" Eli asked.

"Probably another messenger from Sir James. Are ye truly worried about being attacked?"

"Nay. If Thea and Willum come with us, we'll have eight. We'll be fine. But I believe we should be no less than eight. Nearly a score attacked the group before. I dinnae like those numbers."

"Is Wenna going to be able to shoot? A shoulder injury could stop ye from shooting for a wee bit." Ysenda looked over to watch Wenna, then looked at Eli. "Are ye jealous that she has found someone before ye? Or do I sense a wee favor of Alaric?" She phrased her questions in such a low tone that no one else could possibly hear her, and Eli was grateful.

"She said she can shoot, that it hit the part that doesn't pull, and I believe 'twas a shallow wound. And nay, I am no' jealous."

She stared at Ysenda, her only sister. Why didn't she trust her sister enough to tell her the truth about her feelings? And what exactly were her feelings? Did she dare tell her they handfasted?

Nay, that would stay her secret, but she could talk to her a wee bit about all that had transpired.

"I do like Alaric better than I did," she blurted out before she could stop herself. "But if ye tell anyone, I'll twist yer nipples until ye scream."

Ysenda nearly choked on the drink she'd

just taken then smiled. "I'm glad, Eli. Ye need someone. It changes yer entire way of looking at things, and in a good way. If ye are just starting to like him, ye'll see that it will get better."

"I hope so, but honestly, every time Grandda tells me he wants me to marry him, I get angry and refuse. And Grandmama told me the same, and I still refused. I dinnae know why it angers me so, but it does."

Ysenda chuckled. "'Tis an easy answer to that. Ye dinnae like being told what to do. I dinnae like it either, but ye were always worse about it. Ignore them and look at him with an open heart. Dinnae lose someone ye could love forever just for spite. Ye may regret it forever. I'll speak with Grandmama and ask her to leave ye to make up yer own mind."

Eli knew her sister was right. "Promise me ye'll keep my secret?"

"I promise."

The door opened and Maitland stepped in and strode over them. "Pack yer things. We're leaving a day early. Sir James said the English are coming. They are out of the castle in force and searching for food for themselves and their beasts. I'll send a message to Dyna to meet us on the road. Stop yer swooning, Tevis and Wenna!" he called to the lovebirds. "We need ye."

Eli was glad to go, but she had one regret.

She wanted Alaric with them. Now.

Alaric woke up bright and early, knowing what was ahead of him that morn. He dressed carefully, repacked his saddle bag in case they left early, brushed his teeth, then headed below stairs for something to eat.

Broc was finishing his porridge, waving to him as soon as he descended the stairs. There were still a few lingering in the hall, so he nodded to them and grabbed a bowl for himself.

Broc said, "They're waiting for ye already."

"I have to fill my belly first. We eat little on patrol." He covered his porridge with honey, then took two quick bites. "Who?"

"The usual. Alasdair was the first one there, so they told me. Be ready." Broc grinned, knowing it would be a good show for everyone when the two met. He chatted on about the lists, but Alaric was distracted thinking about Alasdair.

He had managed to avoid his cousin for a long time. He couldn't do it any longer. He chatted with a few others before finishing his food. His mother came over and said, "Come back to see us later? I hear ye are wanted in the lists. I may need yer help getting yer sire out here again. He hates staying in his bedchamber."

He stood, finished with his porridge, gave his mother a kiss on her cheek and said, "I'll be back to help ye, Mama. Whatever ye need." He and Broc headed toward the lists, his weapon clean and sharpened. He loved the Grant lists because he had so many fond memories of all he'd learned here. And all the cousins. Uncle Finlay, Alick, Paden, Broc, Uncle Connor, and Hagen.

His brothers, Els and Jowell. But then there was Alasdair and Uncle Jake. No fond memories there.

He had to find a way to avoid Alasdair.

As soon as he stepped onto the training field, he was approached by three of his cousins—Broc, Alick, and Alasdair.

Alasdair looked like he could be Uncle Connor's son as easily as Uncle Jake's. He was the spitting image of their grandfather, though he did not have Connor's height. But Alasdair's shoulders were massive, which Alaric had always envied. His sire had told him to work out in the lists more, and he'd find the same would happen to him. And though it had happened slowly, Alaric's muscles had grown bulkier the more he worked. That was one reason he'd always been willing to spar, though he preferred to train the young guards.

But not Alasdair. After all that had transpired in the past, Alaric struggled with using his sword against Alasdair. It just didn't seem right. Alasdair had lost his father over ten years ago, but the circumstances of Uncle Jake's death stuck in Alaric's mind, as he was certain it did Alasdair's as well.

Jake had died when he'd been training in the lists. He'd just dropped to the ground, dying instantly. Aunt Brenna and Aunt Jennie had said his heart was too big for his body, that his heartbeat had always been off a wee bit. But had they said that out of kindness? He didn't know.

No one would ever know for sure why Uncle

Jake had died that day. But the memory had haunted Alaric ever since.

Alaric thought of his father in the keep, struck only with the bad luck of a broken bone. He'd seen both his sire and his older brother struck down in moments. His feelings then had given him a new appreciation for all that Alasdair had dealt with.

He didn't wish to spar with his cousin. So he took charge of the situation.

"Broc, ye first. I'm ready whenever ye are." Then he'd spar with his Alick. He hoped the noon meal would be called by the time they finished, and he could stay far away from Alasdair.

He and Broc faced off, their blades ringing out when they struck, drawing a crowd of spectators. Everyone liked to watch any of Alex's heirs battle, because they were all so skilled. Which of them was the best swordsman was a common topic of debate in the clan.

Broc had improved quite a bit since they'd last faced each other, but Alaric still held the advantage. He was about to swing for another blow when Broc's ankle turned. He hopped on one foot, holding his hand up to halt the fight. They were using real blades, so no one wished to get hurt or worse yet, strike a cousin down. Alaric lowered his sword immediately and stepped back.

Alasdair said, "Step out, Broc. I'll take yer place."

And there was no backing out of this one.

Alasdair came at him with the famous sideways move of their grandfathers, but Alaric knew how to block it. The two blades met with a powerful clang, the sound drawing cheers from the spectators. The sweat rolled down the side of his face even though the air was chilled.

The two parried, one blow after another blocked, Alaric now heaving from the exertion of swinging his heavy sword, and he had many more swings than Alasdair had, thanks to his fight with Broc. But his cousin's breaths came as fast as his.

Alaric swung his sword over his head, but Alasdair blocked Alaric's blow easily. Alaric swung in a full circle and brought the flat of his blade against Alasdair's sword, catching it hard enough to knock his cousin to the ground and send his sword tumbling.

A figure pushed through the gathered clan members. Dyna, and she looked to be in a hurry.

"Alaric! We must go!" she shouted.

Alaric offered his hand to Alasdair, helping him to his feet.

"Well done, Alaric," Alasdair said.

"My thanks. Ye fought well, too." Alaric forced himself to exchange the courtesies, though his instinct was to sheathe his sword and run. Dyna's timing couldn't have been better, giving him an excuse to leave the lists and ignore the obvious truth.

While he was glad to see his cousin was hale and hadn't been hurt, in his heart, this challenge had convinced him of something he'd considered for a long time.

Alaric was cursed.

CHAPTER EIGHTEEN

A GROUP OF SIX—ELI, Maitland, Wenna, Tevis, Thea, and Willum—rode out from Ramsay land that day, stopping at the cave Eli and Alaric had found as a good meeting place.

"I hope Dyna and Alaric will meet us here," Maitland said.

"I hope so," Eli said. "I'm glad to have ye, Thea and Willum, but we need as many as we can get."

Maitland had stopped at Menzie land and taken a shoulder of smoked boar from the stores to provision them that eve and beyond, and they sat on a log, sharing the flavorful meat, dried fruit, and a loaf of bread, fresh from the oven that morning.

The sound of horses approaching pushed them all to their feet and grabbing for their various weaponry, only to find it was Alaric and Dyna.

The strangest feelings coursed through Eli when she saw Alaric. First it was a wee twinge of happiness in her chest, then a clenching in her belly that she equated to being battle ready. Either could be from Dyna's arrival, she supposed, but the awakening of her nether parts she could only attribute to Alaric Grant.

He dismounted and strode toward them, his swagger going right to the female parts he'd awakened not long ago. His long blond hair had been blown by the wind, but he still looked handsome as hell.

She'd never tell him so. She had sudden visuals of some of the things they'd done together, and it put a smile on her face. Another thing she'd never admit to anyone, especially him—she'd imagined what their bairns might look like. The thought had first arisen when she'd realized that he might have gotten her with child. But even when her courses had come, the idea had refused to pass.

Since they both had green eyes, she was pretty sure their bairn would be green-eyed, but would it be a lad or a lassie? Brown hair or blond like Alaric's? Perhaps a lovely blend.

Alaric just nodded toward her as a greeting, the same as he gave the others. "Hope ye are all well and willing to share yer dinner."

He helped himself to a piece of meat then took a seat on the log opposite Eli. She'd hoped he'd sit next to her, but then she realized it was probably better to keep their distance if she wanted to keep their secret. After all, this was going to be battle time, not the time to be negotiating their handfasting nor creeping away for private time. If he had sat next to her, everyone around them would be thinking of that possibility again.

She was sure that was the only reason he hadn't taken the empty spot next to her.

Dammit to hell, but here she was thinking like a swooning fool.

Dyna saved her from saying anything embarrassing. "Tell me what ye heard, Maitland, and what the plan is."

"Sir James sent word that he'd like assistance. There is a force of English soldiers trying to raid cattle in the Borderlands and a small group of Gascon soldiers searching the fertile farmland along the River Teviot. He mentioned three different areas he'd like patrolled—Coldstream, the lands of Quarrell, and Skaithmuir down to Ettrick Forest. He thinks the soldiers have spread out, so he's asking our assistance in covering more territory. Once we are in the area, we will split up in pairs, one archer and one swordsman."

"Then we move on at first light," Dyna said. "We'll find the bloody bastards."

They finished their meal, and everyone scattered, leaving Eli and Alaric alone at the fire.

"How is yer family? Yer brother any better? And how is yer sire faring, Alaric?" She surely did feel badly for all the suffering his family was dealing with at present.

"My father is healing. He still cannae walk, but Aunt Jennie came and straightened his bone the best she could. She thinks he'll be able to walk again in a moon or two, if he follows her orders. My brother has awakened, I'm glad to say."

"Did he talk with ye about the fall? Did it make ye feel better about no' causing the incident?"

He threw the core of the apple he'd been eating into the fire, then gave her a look of regret. "Nay.

Els cannae talk yet. He just looked at me and smiled. He can move, but is too weak to walk yet. And when I tried to apologize, he got angry."

"I'm sorry to hear that." Hell but looking at Alaric made her want him. He was so good looking, and right now he looked vulnerable, as if he needed an embrace.

"Look, I know we have an odd situation and when this is over, we should talk again, but ye dinnae wish to get involved with me. So dinnae fear I will say anything while we are on patrol."

She gave him a puzzled look. "What the hell are ye talking about?"

"Ye know. Look. I'm going to set ye free. Forget the handfasting. Ye are better without me."

"So I dinnae get a say in this? Ye decided for me?"

"Ye said ye didnae mean it and didnae want to handfast in the first place. I coerced ye because of my grandsire."

She could see the slight tic in his jaw, telling her he was upset about more than what was happening at the moment. What had happened on Grant land?

"Nay, ye dinnae coerce me."

"I did. Seems like it's my decision to release ye and not hold ye to a promise ye didnae make willingly."

That pissed her off, so she stood up and stepped closer, her voice going into a low whisper. "Nay, ye dinnae make any decisions for me. I make my own."

"Fine. But we are done," he said, gritting his

teeth, the line of his jaw still ticking. "Ye should stay far away. I do nothing but hurt people."

Maitland interrupted their conversation. "Trouble between ye two?"

"Nay," Eli replied. "We're fine."

"No trouble," Alaric confirmed.

"Good, because if we split up, ye two are together. But I think ye know that. Alaric, I didn't get the chance to hear how Els is faring. What news do ye have?"

Alaric stepped away to speak with Maitland. Eli headed into the woods to take care of her needs. She didn't know what the hell had gotten into Alaric, but it seemed their short relationship was over.

Fine with her. She had absolutely no feelings for him at all. Except anger that he'd made the decision on his own.

She returned to the fire and sat down on a log with a huff, trimming her nails with a small knife. Thea came and sat down next to her.

"Men can be fools sometimes."

"God's teeth, but ye speak the truth." Alaric couldn't hear her blasphemy, so she used it freely. Perhaps she'd start to use it more often.

"And I care no' what he says, he does like ye. I can see it in his eyes. He didnae look happy just now though. Anything I can help with?" Thea put her hand on Eli's and gave it a squeeze, a much friendlier gesture than her own sister had offered.

"Unless ye can make men stop being arseholes, then nay, probably no'." She sighed and put her blade away. "Ye and Willum got together quickly. Did that bother ye, Thea?"

Thea shook her head emphatically. "But we were involved in those attacks. He was always there to help me, and it developed from there. If no' for the patrols, we'd probably not be together."

"The same for Ysenda and Lewis. She said it was all because of the avalanche. So strange." Eli had to admit that the two were perfect for each other. She'd thought it a sure mismatch until she got to know Lewis better. And she'd never seen her sister happier.

"And Brin and Ceit. And Isla and Grif being locked up together. And Wulf kidnapping Reyna. Dinnae despair. If ye two are destined to be together, the patrol will take care of it for ye. It has an odd way of doing that."

There it was—that word *destiny* again.

Bloody hell.

CHAPTER NINETEEN

A LARIC CURSED HIMSELF all the next
day. He'd been rude to Eli, but he hadn't
been able to help it. All he'd seen when he'd
lain down to sleep were different sets of eyes
bouncing around—Els's when he'd gotten angry
and Alasdair's when he'd knocked him on his
arse. And he hated to admit it, but Alasdair's
eyes were exactly the same as Uncle Jake's eyes.

He was cursed for sure, and no woman should
be with him.

They reached the Borderlands in the middle of
the following day. According to the crofters and
others they spoke to, Sir James Douglas was not
far from Ettrick Forest. They found him and his
men about an hour later.

"Sir James," Maitland said. "How can we help?"

Douglas, determination evident in his dark eyes,
stood tall, his body slender but broad-shouldered.
He glanced back over the open meadow at his
men, probably two score at least, before he spoke,
pushing strands of his dark hair back from his
face. "The Scots blockade has been more than
successful in keeping rations from Edwards troops

at Berwick. I've been told they have killed their horses for meat just to stay alive. But that has had consequences for us, as well. We're getting reports of raiding and looting from many different areas, but I can only send my men so many places. If ye would patrol along the River Teviot, it would be most helpful."

"We'd be honored to assist. Any specifics as to where we should go along the river?" Dyna asked.

"If you go to Coldstream, Skaithmuir, and Quarrell, that would be a great help to us. I'll remain in this general area, so if ye come across any English raiders and need assistance, call for me. I have thirty men close at hand. I will wait for yer return before we go too far." Sir James clasped Maitland's shoulder. "And we are more than grateful for your archers."

Dyna led their group off to a clearing to make plans. "Alaric and Eli, Skaithmuir. Thea and Willum to Quarrel, Tevis and Wenna to Coldstream. Maitland and I will go between these three areas. If ye see any Gascon or English soldiers, dinnae engage with them. Get a count and advise us of what ye have seen. We will confer with Sir James before deciding how to attack."

"Ye'll have to point us in that direction, Maitland," Alaric said. "I dinnae know where Skaithmuir is." He wasn't foolish enough to protect his pride just to get lost in the Borderlands surrounded by starving Englishmen. Even if they didn't engage, he needed to be able to report back on what they found on their share of the patrol.

"We'll head to the river and follow it. I know a good crossroads there where we can plan to meet. The river will lead us to the fertile farmlands, the most likely place to find the soldiers."

They mounted up, and Maitland led the way. Alaric tried to identify landmarks as they rode.

He pulled his horse abreast of Dyna and said in a low voice, "Mayhap Eli should go with ye, and I can go with Maitland."

Dyna's reaction was swift. "Ye are daft if ye think I'm going to send two archers separately from two swordmen. We need to be in pairs or all together."

"True. Then I'll travel with ye and Eli can go with Maitland." Alaric pretended to stare off in the distance while she thought about his proposal.

"If ye'd paid attention, ye would have noticed that Maitland and I are traveling between the three groups. Know ye the three areas, Alaric?"

He sighed and said, "Of course not."

"Then ye know my answer. I suspect it willnae matter for long, because we will eventually join Sir James's force when we take on the English. But for now, we match up. What the bloody hell is in yer head, Alaric?"

Alaric didn't know how to explain what was in his heart, but he trusted Dyna. She knew exactly what had taken place. "Did ye no' see what happened before we left Grant land?"

"I saw ye knocked Alasdair on his arse. What does that have to do with anything?"

He hated that he had to explain this to her. "Can ye no' see, Dyna? I'm cursed. Els, Da,

Alasdair?" He didn't mention the first sign of his curse, which had caused him more pain than any.

"Ye think ye have anything to do with their conditions? Well, ye did knock Alasdair on his arse. 'Tis true. I cannae argue that. But half the sparring matches in the lists end up that way, as ye well know. And ye didnae cause yer sire's and brother's injuries at all. Stop thinking that way."

Alaric was not going to give up easily. She had to see the truth of it. "Ye'll be putting Eli at risk by matching her with me."

"Get that shite out of yer head, Grant, or I'll knock it out. Your father's and brother's problems are *not* your fault. Stop thinking like that when ye are going into battle, or ye will cause injuries. Yer own."

Alaric didn't know what to say. He knew the truth, but she wasn't going to believe him.

"And the other was not yer fault either!"

He frowned, then nodded, moving his horse back. A short time later, Maitland said, "Skaithmuir. That way, Alaric and Eli. Go and report back here in an hour. If we arenae here, then wait under that tree." He pointed to a huge oak that even Alaric knew would make a good landmark.

Eli nodded her agreement. They rode off, leaving the others behind. Alaric vowed they would only talk about their assignment, not his curse nor their future.

"Ye arenae cursed, ye daft idjit." Eli said, actually leaning over to smack him on the shoulder.

"What the hell? Ye were listening to my

conversation with Dyna?" He was furious. How the hell had the wee witch overheard the conversation? The wee, beautiful witch. Hellfire, but he'd never seen her look more stunning. Tight plait, sitting her horse perfectly, tight leggings molded just so to her sweet arse. And now that he knew exactly how perfectly formed her breasts were, he was ruined. If he didn't stop looking at her, he'd have a hard-on for sure.

"I couldn't help but overhear. I was directly in front of the two of ye. And what else was I supposed to do as I rode? And why the bloody hell do ye think ye are cursed? Just because yer brother and father were hurt? There have been plenty of people hurt in my clan, and no one blames themselves. Stop thinking the world revolves around ye."

That comment pissed him off. "There are more than those two. I was just sparring with my cousin and knocked him on his arse. I could have killed him just because I took too wide a swing at him. And there have been others. At least ye dinnae have to deal with a curse."

They followed the path approaching the river, and the area was deserted—no English soldiers, or anyone else, to be seen. In fact, they'd seen nothing but open meadow for the most part. The area was lacking in forestry compared to the Highlands. But there were also no farms, no huts, no villagers. Nothing to draw the soldiers, unless they wished to fish in the river.

Eli's eyes blazed in fury. "Dammit it all to hell and back, but I do have a curse and his name is Logan Ramsay. Ye know what he thinks? He thinks I should marry ye. That we should make this big alliance like Aunt Brenna and Uncle Quade did. And so does my grandmother."

"And ye told him what happened between us?" He hadn't expected that news. Logan wanted him to marry his granddaughter?

"Nay, I didnae tell anyone. Too embarrassing."

"Ye're embarrassed? About me and what we did? If ye did no' like it, why'd ye beg for it? Ye are such a stubborn lass. And ye curse like a sailor. Why do ye no' just say nay, if the thought upsets ye so much?"

"I've been saying nay for a long time, but they keep nagging me. I told them I'll pick my own husband and they can stay out of my life. 'Tis no one's say but mine. And who else did ye ever hurt?"

Alaric huffed at her blatant change of subject. "It doesnae matter."

"It does matter if ye wish for me to believe ye are cursed. It surely wasnae yer fault that two horses fell. That was just because of the weather. Or are ye God and can control the weather now? And as far as Alasdair goes, if ye cannae knock someone on their arse, ye shouldnae be out here."

"Oh, does that make it right? Sure, I'll accept that. Knocking someone on their arse isnae a big deal, perhaps, but it is if ye kill someone. Does that fit with yer finicky rules, Queenie?'

"God's bollocks, dinnae call me Queenie."

"But ye act like one. Always barking orders. Ye have to make all yer own decisions. And ye promised to stop being blasphemous. That didnae last long, did it?"

"I'll curse however I want. Ye try to tell me what to do. I'll curse. No reason to respect yer wishes if ye made a decision for me without talking about it."

"Ye are only one person I made a decision about, and it was what ye wanted anyway. Maybe ye should make decisions for everyone. Would that make ye happy, Queenie?"

"Nay, stop calling me that. And what the hell are ye speaking of? Who would want anyone to make decisions for them?"

"Queenie."

"Stop it. God's arse."

"Or what? Ye have no power over me. Have ye ever killed someone, Queenie?"

"Stop calling me that, or I'll make yer two sacs into four when ye least expect it."

Alaric was stunned at that comment. He knew she was crude, but that was worse than he'd ever heard before. He fought the urge to put his hand in front of his bollocks. She'd think it was hysterical, and that knowledge gave him the strength to resist.

"Wait," she said, looking confused. "Ye killed an Englishman so ye think ye are cursed? Ye are supposed to kill the enemy."

"It wasnae the enemy I killed!"

She stopped her horse to face him.

"Ye cannae stop yer horse, Queenie. Keep going. We have an assignment to complete." The river flowed languidly beside them and the path spooled out empty before them. Where the hell was everyone? Fortunately, there were no English to be seen yet. But for trees dotting the landscape here and there, it was a desolate area.

"Nay," she replied, her voice quiet. "I'll not go another step until ye tell me who ye killed. Ye killed someone ye know? On purpose?"

"Nay," he answered, turning toward her. "No' on purpose. It was an accident, but it truly shows that I'm cursed."

"Who?'

"It doesnae matter who. Move yer horse." He couldn't even say the words. They were too painful.

"Who? Who did ye kill?"

"Leave it be. Ye dinnae need to know. 'Tis. Not. Yer. Concern."

"It is, if ye're using this curse foolishness to make decisions about my life. Who. Did. Ye. Kill?"

Alaric cursed under his breath, but the lass was as stubborn as anyone he knew. He believed her that she would not let up until he confessed, so he might as well tell her the awful truth.

"My uncle. All right? I killed Uncle Jake."

CHAPTER TWENTY

ELI GASPED. SHE'D never heard anything of the sort. Jake Grant had died over a decade ago, but she'd never heard that his death was anything but natural, let alone that he'd been killed by someone in their clan.

They'd all been told that he just dropped, that his death was instantaneous, and they had no idea why but it probably had something to do with his heart. How could Alaric be responsible?

Sympathy blossomed inside her.

"And I dinnae want yer pity," Alaric growled.

"Tell me more. Please, Alaric. What happened?" She reached for him, but he held his hand up to stop her.

"Hush. I hear something." He glanced over at a small copse not far from them.

She did too.

They waited quietly to determine if what they heard was an animal or men. It only took a moment to know for sure.

Men's voices. Since there was little more than scattered bits of vegetation and trees dotting the rolling hills of farmland along the vast riverbank, it shouldn't be hard for them to locate the voices.

Alaric pointed to a thick cluster of bushes off to the side. "Dismount," he whispered.

They both swung as quietly as possible to the ground and left the path. Eli wished their tack didn't creak and jingle so much. They waited, motionless, until they were certain of what they heard.

"I can hear men talking," Eli said softly, "and I'm certain I heard them say Douglas's name."

"I agree." Alaric pointed in the direction of the voices. "That way. Quietly. You count and I'll listen. Stay hidden behind the trees."

They looped their reins around a convenient branch, then made their way down the line of trees, his hand in hers, until Alaric held a finger to his lips. Eli stood directly behind him, still gripping his hand. She peeked through the trees and caught her breath.

English soldiers, and a lot of them. Too many. It looked like a full troop of men in tattered old uniforms.

One man spoke, and his bearing marked him as the leader of the force. "Douglas is looking for us. I say we take him on and wipe out his paltry group of soldiers. Then we can steal all the cattle we need to fortify our stores back at Berwick."

"The Scots won't be able to stand against us, Sir Edmund," the man to his right said.

She had no idea who Sir Edmund was, but they were clearly English. Weaponry, clothing, and accents all pointed to an English force. And they were from Berwick. But beyond what any passing glance would see was something else. The entire force looked exhausted. Dirty, worn and ripped clothing, pitiable weaponry. They hardly represented the fearsome English force she'd expected to see.

"I'm hungry. Let's go find the bastards. Mount up," Sir Edmund said.

Alaric gave Eli a wide-eyed look.

She was busy counting. The soldiers were arranged in small groups of five or so, so she counted the groups. Thirty-five, forty... Hellfire but there was at least another score of the scurvy bastards.

Alaric pointed back the way they'd come, and they crept off, making it back to their horses. He tossed her up on hers, a finger to his lips to keep quiet. They turned together toward the crossroads where their group had split up. Once out of earshot of the English, they kicked their horses into a faster pace.

They made it to the crossroads without saying a word. Dyna was there waiting for them.

"Did ye learn something?" she asked.

"There's an English cavalry squadron less than ten miles along the river. They're talking of seeking out Sir James and attacking the Scots. Someone named Sir Edmund seems to be their commanding officer." Alaric stroked his mount's neck. The black warhorse could have easily outpaced Eli's mount, but he'd stayed close to her.

Hearing Alaric's report to Dyna made her heart pound harder than it had even when they'd seen the English soldiers. Hellfire, but Eli had the feeling she was about to experience her first full battle against the English.

"Keep the rest for Sir James. We must hurry. Maitland will know where we have gone."

The group of three hadn't traveled far when they encountered Sir James with his two score of fighting Scotsmen behind him. Far more able-bodied than the English they'd just left, the men were anxious for battle, their weapons cleaned and ready to take on anyone who dared challenge them.

"Ye have news?" Douglas asked. "I've been searching everywhere for the slimy bastards." His men moved closer to overhear the conversation.

"Aye," Dyna said, nodding to Alaric, who repeated all he'd heard.

"How many?"

"Around three score from my count," Eli said.

One of the men behind Douglas said, "Since when can a lass count? And why do ye have two lasses with ye at all?"

Eli whipped out her bow and nocked an arrow so fast every man fell silent in shock. "Say it again, and I'll show ye why I'm here."

"Ye are a pretty one, I'll give ye that, lass." He wore a wide grin and held his arms out to his side. "Come to me." He placed his hands in front of his bollocks and rubbed himself.

Before she could voice her own retort, Alaric said, "Touch her and I'll kill ye with my bare hands."

Sir James drew his sword and pointed it at his men. "Any more insults, and ye'll have to deal with me. If ye werenae a fool, ye'd recognize the Ramsay plaid and ye'd know they train the best archers in Scotland. Shut yer mouth or dismount and walk home. I'll no' have any under my command who disrespects a woman or an ally."

The man said nothing, so Eli lowered her bow and arrow.

"I'd be wary," Dyna warned. "Her grandmother trained her by teaching her how to hit a man between his bollocks."

Eli couldn't hide her grin as a quarter of the men behind Douglas placed their hands in front of their privates. She drawled, "So ye'd all prefer an arrow through yer fighting hand than yer bollocks? And ye think men are the smarter ones."

Dyna snorted.

"Enough," Sir James said. "How long before they arrive?"

"Not long." They described the area where they'd seen the group, giving them all the details they remembered.

"Lead me there. My men are seasoned fighters. We've been defending our land for over ten years. We'll not back down now, not on my marches." He mounted and pointed for Dyna to lead the way.

They'd not gone far when the sounds of horse hooves in the distance rang out. Sir James said to his men, "Half of you hide behind the ford." He waited for the approach of the English forces.

She witnessed the scene unfold in front of her,

this knight in full armor who waited to see if the English would attack.

"We will fight?" Dyna asked.

"Aye." Sir James pointed to a man behind them, who raised a pole that had been strapped to his saddle, unfurling a flag of white with a blue band marked by three white stars.

"These are my marches," Sir James said. "We will fight, even though we are outnumbered. I hope the rest of yer group will join us."

Maitland and the others came galloping across the land near the river, joining them. Alaric repeated his scouting report. When he mentioned Sir Edmund's name, Maitland nodded.

"'Tis the Gascon knight Sir Edmund Cailhau, Sir James."

"The bastard," Sir James said. He shouted orders to his men, arranging them the way he wanted, to best defend against the larger number.

Dyna shouted to Eli, Wenna, and Thea. "Follow me! Into the trees. All four of us."

Eli grabbed her weapons and raced after Dyna. A pair of squires took the four women's horses well behind the lines for safety. Alaric followed her to a tree and lifted her into the branches, but not before leaning over to whisper in her ear, "I love ye, lassie mine. God be with ye." And he was gone, back on his own mount, his sword unsheathed, and the Grant war whoop echoing across the vast meadow.

Dammit to hell, but she would not cry. She made sure to track Dyna, Thea, and Wenna, marking their locations. Thea was in the same tree as she was while Dyna and Wenna were each in their own a little farther along the road.

"Ye fine, Eli? We'll be fine here," Thea said. "Think like Grandmama taught ye and shoot to kill."

Chapter Twenty-One

PERHAPS HE SHOULDN'T have said what he had, but the words bubbled out of his insides before he helped her into the tree. None of them knew how this battle would end, and he had to make his feelings known. Hell, but she was a beauty, and she'd felt like heaven his arms... Well. He had to pray he'd have the chance to experience it again.

They had to send the English running first, then he'd apologize to Eli for yelling at her earlier in the day.

Willum took up his position next to him. "They're everywhere. Pay attention, Grant, and Godspeed to all of us! Thea! I love ye!"

The archers were lined up perfectly with the English cavalry racing toward them. Within moments, arrows sluiced through the air, taking several of the English out before they ever reached the Scots.

"Son of a bitch, but they can shoot!" one of Douglas' men shouted just as two more soldiers fell. "She got one right in the heart! Where did they train?"

Maitland laughed and said, "Gwyneth Ramsay. And they'll save yer arse more than once this day. Ye'll see."

Then Sir James's voice rang out. "Charge!"

Their horses leapt forward, closing the distance between Scots and English in the blink of an eye.

Alaric found himself in the middle of the biggest battle he'd ever been in, the ring of clashing swords echoing across the meadow. There was no place to hide, but the English were not strong.

They had poor weapons, and their blows were slow and weak—evidence of their starvation. But still, they outnumbered the Scots.

Every time Alaric knocked one to the ground, another one replaced him. There were more English than he and Eli had seen. Where the hell had they all come from? He swung and swung his blade until all the muscles in his back were strained and screaming for him to stop.

But he couldn't.

Out of the corner of his eye, he caught the archers dropping to the ground and running to trees that were closer to the fighting. One of the English soldiers went after them, smart enough to realize they should be taken out, but too stupid to think through how. An arrow from one of the women—Alaric didn't see which—knocked him off his mount before he was even close. The lasses scrambled into trees and out of reach.

"Come on, ye rat bastards!" He laughed a little wildly. Loki had said how good it felt to call the English that term. He was right.

He took two more out, one with a stab to his

belly and the other a hit on the side of his head with the flat of his sword, knocking him off his mount.

The thud of his landing brought Els's fall to mind.

A group of three Englishmen, shields held over their heads, went straight for the trees where the lasses perched.

"Willum, come with me!" Alaric shouted.

Eli's voice rang out. "Ye want one between yer bollocks, ye hedge-born piece of filth?" She fired, catching one soldier in the leg, though he managed to keep his seat. His yell of pain made one of the others lower his shield, and Eli's next arrow hit him in the chest, knocking him to the ground in a heap. Willum took care of the third man with a swift slash across his middle.

The injured man must have been driven mad by pain or battle. He jumped off his horse and ran at Eli's tree, his sword raised over his head and screaming like a banshee.

Eli got him exactly where she told him she would.

He screamed and fell to the ground, writhing in pain. Alaric dismounted and put the man out of his misery.

"Well done, lasses," Maitland called.

Alaric took a moment to catch his breath before swinging back into the saddle and turning back to the melee. Sir James, his position marked by his standard-bearer, looked to be going after the leader of the English, Sir Edmund. The two met and their swords thrust and parried. Others tried to take Sir James down, but Alaric pushed them back. Maitland joined him, protecting their leader while he fought. Alaric lost track of time in the constant chaos, but Sir James finally took down the English knight.

A roar went up, and for a moment, the English surged toward where their leader had fallen. Alaric was hard-pressed to keep them back. But then something broke in the English force. Some of the English turned tail, and the Scots pushed the remaining fighters back, across ground littered with bodies. Bit by bit, the fighting eased.

Alaric glanced about, seeing Tevis, Willum, and Maitland ahead of him. He breathed a sigh of relief when he set his eyes on Eli and the other lasses, and he returned to what remained of the battle.

Maitland was up near the front of the line, fighting the few remaining English who refused to turn tail with their comrades. Alaric saw a flash of steel, and Maitland yelled in pain, his sword falling to the ground.

Alaric raced forward, getting his horse in front of Maitland's to block any attack while his friend was unarmed. Maitland had pulled out a small dagger, but that would not help against a sword.

Alaric took up the fight with the soldier who had wounded Maitland, striking him in his chest. Blood spouted as he fell off his horse.

"Maitland, I'll get yer weapon. Get away, and I'll handle the stragglers."

The last bit of fighting did not last long. The rest of the English soldiers turned tail, leaving the field of battle.

Alaric turned his horse around to follow Maitland who was staring at the ground and leaning dangerously to one side. "Menzie, stop."

"My sword. I cannae find my sword."

Any Scot would feel the same need to find his weapon. The feel of your own hilt was better than any other.

"Stop. I'll find yer sword, but I must slow the bleeding in yer arm first. It's bleeding heavily."

Maitland looked at him, very confused.

Alaric didn't like that, so he grabbed the reins of Maitland's horse, leading him to a spot to the side so he could tend to his wound.

Maitland fell off his horse before he could get to him.

CHAPTER TWENTY-TWO

ELI WAS LOOKING for her next target when Dyna yelled, "Stop! It's over. Let's retrieve as many arrows as we can salvage and find our men."

Thea jumped down from the tree and followed Dyna into the sea of the fallen, desperately looking for Willum, Eli was sure. Wenna called out to Tevis, but got no answer.

Where the hell was Alaric?

Eli found her way into the middle of the field, dead and injured men everywhere, the sounds of wailing voices nearly too much to bear. She'd noticed aches in various spots on her body when she was in the tree, but she's ignored them because she had no choice.

A strong pain in her shoulder nearly brought her to her knees. Her hand reached up to check for blood, but none was there. Who had been hurt? Her gaze took in the entire air, drawing a breath of shock.

Stunned by the view, she scanned one area of the field then another, the sea of bodies overwhelming her while her hand still protected her shoulder. She made her way through the battlefield, doing her best not to step on anyone, and her eyes traveled from one face to the next. Some were dead with their eyes still open, others struggling to move, reaching for anything or anyone.

A hand tugged on her ankle but she yanked away, a dying Englishman begging her. "Help me."

Where was Alaric? Where were Willum and Maitland and Tevis? All she saw were Englishmen—dead, nearly dead, or severely wounded.

Stabs of pain assaulted her, and she jerked in reaction to each one. Every time she felt a new pain in one part of her body or another, she glanced down to see a man holding or bleeding from that part of his body, looking to her for salvation.

Her chest hurt, nay, her head, nay, her foot, nay, her shoulder. She grabbed her hair and tugged on it, the tears she'd held inside for so long pouring down her cheeks in buckets.

She couldn't take any more.

Where was Alaric?

She sobbed in wrenching spurts as she continued across the field. There was blood everywhere, and the stench of death overpowered her senses.

One man grabbed her leg. "Take it out. Ye put it there." His words came out in an odd, strangled way.

He had an arrow straight through his cheek. A second arrow protruded from his flank. "Take it out!"

She hurried forward. "Alaric? Where are ye?"

She'd known that any battle would involve death, but she'd never imagined the reality of being so close to it. And it wasn't just the visual. Death assaulted every one of her senses. The screams dropped to wails and then to odd, raspy breathing before they finally stopped.

"Alaric? Please, Alaric."

She loved Alaric. He said he'd loved her. Now she knew her own heart. If she came upon a body and it belonged to him, she'd never be right again. Each time she searched the face of a fallen body, she prayed it wouldn't be Alaric. He was the only one for her.

He'd said he loved her. *Her!*

More bodies. More blood. More death.

She moved blindly to any bare spot, hoping to avoid any of the not-yet-dead, but one sat up quickly and grabbed her hips, tugging her toward him. "I'll kill ye, lass."

Falling to the ground on top of the brute, she used her fist to deliver a blow to his face, then pushed away and kicked him in the belly, giving her the time to scramble in the other direction so she could get back to her feet.

A sudden jolt of pain in her leg made her knee buckle. She glanced down to see a sword wound that had nearly severed the man's leg. By the amount of blood around him, he'd died quickly.

She pushed forward, wishing the sounds away. Closing her eyes at the things she saw, pinching her nose to stop the assault on her nostrils.

Go away. Go away. Go away.

One of Douglas's men called out to her. "Help me, please. I'll live if ye get me away."

She couldn't see his wound at first, but a sudden sharp pain told her where to look. She pulled his arm back and stared at a slash across his hip, still bleeding heavily.

"I can help ye. I can. I need something to help ye." She stood up and searched the area. "Alaric! Dyna! Anyone!"

Voices called out to her, moans and whimpers. Last words uttered before a life fizzled away.

"Alaric!" Where was he? She began to move faster, the need for this man whom she trusted and loved so strong now that it overpowered her. There were more men trying to stand, more crying out for help.

Sir James made his way through the dead, looking for his men. She pointed him toward the man she'd promised to help. Then she saw a small group off to the side of the field. Were they not in blue and red plaids?

"Alaric?"

A hand grabbed her heel while another man called out to her. "Help me, please."

Her tears overflowed again, and she wanted nothing more than to escape the horror around her.

The man gripped her foot so hard that she fought to stay upright.

She did the only thing she could do.

Eli tipped her head back and screamed and screamed and screamed.

CHAPTER TWENTY-THREE

ALARIC FOUND MAITLAND'S sword and carried it to him, the sight of it settling the other man immediately.

"Many thanks to ye, Grant," Maitland said, trying to push himself up but failing.

Alaric cleaned off both Maitland's and his own sword on a clump of weeds off to one side. It would do for now. He had to tend Maitland's wound before he did anything else.

Alaric fetched a clean tunic from his saddlebag, tore it into strips, and wrapped them tight around Maitland's arm.

"Where are the others?" Maitland asked. He seemed less confused than he had before, and Alaric was grateful.

"Dyna's coming, and I think she has Willum and Thea with her."

"How bad is it, Alaric?" Dyna called as she hurried toward them.

"He'll survive, but he needs stitching."

"I'm fine," Maitland said. "Where are the others?"

Willum joined them in time to answer. "Tevis and Wenna are right behind us. We're only missing Eli."

Alaric's heart stuttered then raced, the sudden thunder in his chest telling him he needed to find Eli. "When did ye see her last? Thea, she was still in the tree with ye?"

"Aye," Dyna answered. "She came down with us, but I noticed she was wandering across the battlefield. I called to her once, but she didn't hear me. She's uninjured. I needed to find ye all first."

"Hell," Alaric cursed. "She's probably confused by all the injuries."

Dyna crossed her arms. "What are ye talking about?"

"She can feel injuries. If someone is severely hurt near her, she feels it in her own body. So she is probably in terrible pain, if she's walking among the bodies. I'll go find her."

A scream rent the air, and he knew it was Eli. "That's her."

He ran, following the sound of her scream. She screamed and screamed and screamed. He zigzagged through the sea of bodies, nearly running into Sir James. He didn't pause, merely nodded as he raced by.

By the time he got to Eli, her face was covered in tears and her eyes were so red they had to be sore. She called his name, and he grabbed her.

"I've got ye, love," he said, hanging tight even as she tried to push him away. It was a moment before she recognized him. When she looked at him, she closed her eyes and wrapped her arms around him, sobbing into his shoulder.

"Ye are hale, Alaric?"

"I am."

"The others?"

"All will live. Maitland may need stitching. None other is even scratched."

"I'll do it."

She stepped back and peered up at him. "I'll help any of the Scots who need help, but I'll no' walk through the bodies again."

He cupped her cheeks and kissed her, a deep kiss to let her know that he meant what he'd said before. When he ended the kiss, he used his thumb to brush away the tears. "Ye *can* cry, lass."

"Don't tell anyone. I was so worried about ye and…" Her breath hitched. "And I love ye too. How do we get to the others? I cannae walk across this field again."

"Ye felt their pain, did ye no'?"

"Aye. It was horrible."

"Come, I'll take ye to Maitland."

He lifted her into his arms. "No more walking past the injured. I'll carry ye to the side."

She rested her head on his shoulder and sighed. Despite his surroundings, Alaric felt as if all was right with him now, with Eli leaning on him and he supporting her. He picked his way to clear ground, then set her down. They walked around the battlefield to Maitland and the others.

By the time they got there, Eli was breathing more easily, and she dropped to Maitland's side to look at his wound. "I can sew it, Maitland. But I dinnae have good tools. And ye know how Aunt Brenna is about making it clean first. What say ye?"

Sir James came behind her and said, "I have a few who need stitching. Can ye help them, too?"

Eli nodded. "I'll try, but I need needle and thread."

Sir James said, "I know a healer not far from here. She will have the tools ye need, and we have enough injuries ye both will have enough to do. Did ye lose any, Menzie?"

"Nay. How many have ye lost?"

"A few. Not as many as the English. I thank ye for yer assistance. I'll gather our men and lead ye to the healer."

Alaric watched Sir James shout instructions to his men, sending them off to find the survivors. He stayed close to Eli, not quite willing to be apart from her yet. He spoke with Dyna while Willum and Tevis helped with the aftermath of the battle.

"How did this battle compare to others, Dyna?" he asked. His arms ached from the weight of his sword and the blows he'd dealt.

"Worse than most. Larger than most. I didnae expect to see that many English. They had more than three score. They must have had another unit join them, though they lost most of them."

Sir James gave a final order, then rejoined them, leading his horse. Just before he mounted, he turned to Maitland and Dyna. "I must say that this battle was one of the most difficult I've ever fought. I am truly indebted to ye for yer assistance. Ye were a blessing to my men."

Sir James led them away from the battlefield. Eli rode double with Alaric on her horse, allowing his to rest after the battle. She was too weak to ride on her own. She'd lost her strength to the battle, though she didn't understand why. She had to admit that letting Alaric take over suited her just fine. Just this once. There were a few things she needed to settle in her mind before they arrived at the healer's cottage.

First of all, she'd cried. "I cried, Alaric."

"Aye. I'd call it sobbing hysterically, but call it as ye wish. 'Tis a most normal thing to do."

"I never cry. And no one else did."

"Thea and Wenna both cried, and I believe Tevis shed a few tears also."

"But no' Dyna. I wonder why." She hated to admit she'd lost all control, but crying had helped her to release the pain and horror from her body.

"Dyna has been in more battles than ye have. Dinnae feel badly about it."

"But ye didnae cry. Why do men no' cry?" She'd never seen her father cry. She'd heard of a few times when Grandsire had cried, but no' often.

"I cry. I didnae cry today because I drained all my tears when I saw my brother lying in that bed and no' moving. The thought of my brother never awakening again was a terrible blow. I cried and I didnae care. Dinnae be embarrassed. Sometimes yer body needs it. And yer mind. It relieves the grip the fear has on yer insides."

She considered his words then said, "I suppose ye are correct."

Her next thought was on the words she'd uttered. And the ones she'd heard from Alaric. "Did ye mean what ye said before the battle started?" She didn't even turn back to look in his eyes because she feared what she'd see. Would he deny his words? Did he truly love her? Or was it something someone said before a battle?

"I did. I know ye dinnae think of it often, but we are handfasted. I expect us to be so for the full year and a day, and married for many years more. I'm sorry for denying ye before. I was upset from all that happened when I went home. The truth is, ye were the only nice thought I had since the accident. I have verra fond memories of our first night together. Ye dinnae mean yer words?"

"I did." The tension in her chest eased once he admitted his feelings were true. No doubt battle had pushed them together, but when it was all over he came for her. When everyone else had gone, Alaric was there. "I'm still trying to comprehend how frantic I felt in the middle of the battlefield. What an awful place."

"Most true. Did ye feel their wounds?"

"Aye. Many of them. I didnae expect it, since I've only felt the pain of loved ones before. I dinnae understand how it happens to begin with, or today specifically. I'm so confused."

He rubbed her arm and said, "Dinnae think on it now, lass. Think on tending Maitland and helping the other Scots where we can, then I'll take ye home to Ramsay land."

"Ye'll go with me?"

"Aye."

"Do ye have a purpose?"

"Aye, I wish to speak with yer parents. I'm no' sure if I've met yer mother."

"I'd be happy to introduce ye." She leaned back against him, content for the moment with the understanding between them.

They came into a small village, and Sir James pointed to a larger cottage that sat behind a line of smaller huts.

"That one in the back. She's always there. Her name is Agnes."

The men who needed help lined up outside the cottage while Sir James, Eli, and Alaric led Maitland inside. Eli introduced herself.

The healer was an older woman who seemed unflappable, given her moderate reaction to news of the battle. Agnes was wide in the hip but had compassionate green eyes. Her hair was black with strands of gray throughout. Her hands were a bit gnarled, but Eli could see how much the woman used them, jars and goblets of various sizes around the chamber, full of ointments and potions, if Eli were to guess.

"Ye are related to Brenna Ramsay?" she asked Eli.

"Aye, Brenna is my aunt."

"My, but ye are a blessed one. And what about Jennie Cameron?" The woman's eyes lit up when she mentioned Aunt Jennie.

"Aye, I know her too." She found a place for Maitland to sit, then worked at cleaning Maitland's wound, choosing her tools carefully before sewing it. The healer gave Maitland a small drink of whisky, which he seemed grateful for.

The first of Douglas's men came in with a large wound on his leg, and Agnes began giving instructions to Thea and Wenna, who'd come inside to assist. Alaric sat across from Maitland, and the two spoke in hushed voices.

Agnes locked over at Eli's work. "Please explain anything ye are doing. The two sisters are the finest healers in all the land. I would love to learn from them. The first question I'll ask is why ye are washing his wound. Has it not begun to clot already? Are ye no' opening it again?"

Eli explained. "Aunt Brenna said she and her sire did a test long ago and the clean wounds healed better. She has a need for cleanliness in all things. Most dinnae feel the way she does, but if ye were in her keep, ye would see that 'tis most clean everywhere. 'Tis Aunt Brenna's way."

She explained a few other things to Agnes as she worked, and she soon had Maitland's wound neatly stitched.

"Have ye planned where we go next?" she asked.

Maitland admired her handiwork. "Many thanks for yer fine care, lass. Ye and Alaric will go to Ramsay land. I am going home to retrieve my verra pregnant wife and take her to Aunt Jennie's to await the bairn. My mother is insisting, and Maeve is pleased to accommodate her. Wenna will go with me—I believe her parents are on Cameron land. Tevis, Thea, and Willum will go with ye. Not sure yet where Dyna is going. But Sir James said there is no need to patrol for a fortnight. This battle will slow the English down. They need to take stock of how many remain in the Borderlands."

"Maitland, before we take our leave, I think we should tell ye something," Alaric said, shooting a glance at Eli. She nodded her agreement. "Eli and I handfasted that night in the cave, and we intend to marry when the time is right."

Maitland chuckled. "I'm not surprised. But may I make a recommendation?"

"Please do," Eli said.

"I wouldn't tell yer sire and grandsire *when* it happened." He gave them both a sly grin. "I'd just say it happened because of the battle. Not a lie, but not as many details. Ye'll stave off any intense questions. Not that Uncle Logan has ever questioned any lads about his daughters or granddaughters…" He arched a brow at Alaric, then Eli.

Alaric scowled, turning to Eli. "Are ye worried he'll no' accept me?"

Maitland said, "He'll accept ye, but he'll also make yer life miserable for a while. Look what he did to poor Cailean, and he adores him."

"He'll be right happy, Alaric," Eli said. "He's been nagging me to marry ye for far too long for him to complain now."

"Just beware," Maitland said, a wide grin crossing his face. "And prepare."

CHAPTER TWENTY-FOUR

WHEN THEY ARRIVED back on Ramsay land, they paused at the turnoff to Thea's parents' house to wish the two farewell.

"Where are the two of ye going to live?" Eli asked.

Thea replied, "Da said he would build us a house behind his work shed. It will be a bit more in the woods, but he promised Willum that he would build one of those sliding ceilings over our bedroom like Uncle Aedan and Aunt Jennie have, so we can sleep under the stars. For now, we sleep in my chamber. I'm sure we'll see ye in the hall. I like to go up for meals on occasion, especially for the big meal at the end of each fortnight. So does Da, and Mama usually follows."

"Take greetings to yer parents," Alaric said, and the remaining three rode on.

Tevis was extra quiet.

"Ye and Wenna have gotten close. Do ye like her enough to ask for her hand?" Alaric asked.

"Aye, but I dinnae think she is ready yet. I think she needs to speak with her mama. We were both a wee bit surprised by the battle, not having as much experience as others. I think I will try to head home to Black Isle, if I can find someone to travel with me."

"I'll be heading home to Grant land shortly. I'll join ye for part of the way."

"I'll let ye know when I leave. My thanks to ye, Alaric."

As soon as he noticed her grandfather headed toward them, Tevis moved on ahead with a wave and a wink, and Eli let him go. She waited for her grandsire to get close enough for her to blurt out her thoughts, other than asking him how he always knew when someone was arriving on Ramsay land.

Uncle Quade used to joke that there were actually two Logans living on Ramsay land, one who patrolled and the other who bossed everyone about.

"Greetings to ye, Grandsire. We handfasted so now ye can be happy and leave us be."

Her grandfather's eyes narrowed as he stopped his horse across the path so they couldn't get past him. "Is that so?" He looked to Alaric who started to speak but the man held his palm up to stop him. "Never mind. I'll speak with ye later."

"That's all ye have to say after all the pestering?" Eli asked.

"Yer grandmother told me to stop pestering, so I was planning on it. The last thing I expected was to see that ye did what I told ye to." His crafty gaze went from one to the other. "Humph."

"What are ye looking for, Grandda?"

"I'm looking to see if ye are lying or if 'tis true.

By his expression, I think 'tis true, but by the expression on yer face, lass, I think ye are lying."

"Ye are accusing me of lying? Truly?"

"Are ye? I havenae accused yet." He lifted his chin, tipping his head back.

"Och! I'm leaving. I need to visit Grandmama."

"Wait!" Her grandfather didn't look pleased at all.

"What? I'm worried about Grandmama. Ye frighten me, Grandda. Is Grandmama hale? Has she improved?"

"Nay, she hasnae improved. So I'm telling ye to visit with her but dinnae pester her. Aunt Brenna is trying different salves and ointments and potions. Naught has worked yet, but she isnae giving up, so dinnae ye give up either."

Logan clicked to his horse, and they rode to the castle together, Alaric reaching over and taking her hand as they rode behind him.

Eli was surprised to see so many inside the gates to greet them. Alaric dismounted and helped her down just before her sister threw herself at her, hugging her tight. She was surprised to find her hands trembling a bit, she guessed from the effects of battle.

"Ysenda? Has something happened that I dinnae no?"

"Nay," her sister replied, stepping back to look her up and down. "I was worried about ye. We heard there was a big battle. That some were injured. Ye werenae? Though ye are shaking. What is wrong?"

"I am fine. Word travels quickly. The only one

of our group who was injured is Maitland. He's on his way to Cameron land. He took a shoulder wound that just needed to be cleaned and stitched, and I took care of it."

"Ye did?" Her sister stepped back and planted her fists on her hips. "Since when are ye a healer?"

"Since no one else could do it."

"She did a fine job sewing up several wounds," Alaric said with a proud nod. "How is yer leg, Ysenda?"

"'Tis fine. Never the same, but 'tis fine." She grabbed her sister's hand to lead her into the keep. "She's home, Da. She's fine."

Her parents were both headed her way, so Eli quickly explained, "We're all well. Alaric and I would like to see Grandmama. Then we can talk. Do ye mind?"

Her father checked both of them over closely, then said, "Aye. I'll take ye to her. She's no' well, lass. Prepare yerself."

She waved to a few others who had come out to see the new arrivals, but she didn't take the time to speak to them.

She paused outside her grandmother's chamber and stared at her father. "Alaric can go with me, Da. Ye dinnae have to."

Her father kissed her forehead and walked away. She steeled herself for whatever she would find, then opened the door.

She hadn't steeled herself enough.

"Grandmama?" The chamber was dark and she could hear slight moaning coming from the mound on the bed. She dropped Alaric's hand and rushed over, falling to her knees to look the dear woman in the eyes.

"Who's there?" her grandmother asked, pushing her blanket away and peering through the darkness.

"Grandmama, 'tis me. Eli. I brought Alaric with me. He wishes to meet ye."

"He's a Grant. I know all the Grants. They're all alike."

"But he doesnae know ye." She reached over and tucked a few stray hairs back from her face, tucking them carefully behind her ears.

Her grandmother peered up at him, tipping her head back to lock on his face. "He is a handsome one. He looks like Jamie and Maddie. Greetings, Alaric."

"'Tis a pleasure to make yer acquaintance, Lady Ramsay."

"Gwyneth. I'm no lady."

"Aye, ye are, Grandmama."

"Gwyneth."

"Gwyneth," Alaric finally said.

"Why is he here?" her grandmother asked.

"Because we handfasted, and he wished to meet ye." Eli squeezed her eyes shut to stop the tears from drenching her cheeks. She hadn't cried in years until the battlefield just days ago, and now she was ready to let the tears flow again. But she didn't wish for her grandmother to see them.

"Ye handfasted before but wouldn't admit it, would ye, lassie?"

Hell, but how had she known?

She couldn't help but giggle. "Ye are always and forever a wise one, Grandmama."

"Congratulations. Take care of my lass, Alaric Grant. Dinnae hurt her or I'll find ye."

"I'll no' hurt her. I love her."

Eli moved over to pull the fur back from the window to let the light in.

"Leave it, Eli."

"Nay, I need to look at ye. Darkness isnae good," she said, wishing to get a true look at her grandmother before she let the fur drop again. Her face was gaunt and flushed, so much that she couldn't' stop herself from reaching over with her hand to touch her forehead and her cheeks.

"Aye, I have the fever bad. Brenna has tried many potions on me, but she cannae get it to go away. Or it stops for an hour or two, then comes back. 'Tis no' good."

"How is yer knee?"

"Swollen, full of green pus, so painful that it tortures me to take care of my needs. I may just start wetting the bed because of it."

Alaric pulled a stool over next to the bed, motioning for Eli to take it. "Gwyneth, I promise to take good care of her. And I must thank ye for helping to raise a feisty lass like Eli. I know ye had much to do with her archery skills, but I think ye helped to form her powerful nature, and 'tis one of the things I love most about her." He kissed Eli's cheek. "I'll meet ye back out in the hall."

Gwyneth waited until Alaric had shut the door behind him before speaking. "Ye like him, lass?"

"I do, Grandmama." Her cheeks heated thinking of how much she liked him.

"And the battle? I heard it was a rough one."

"Horrific. Dead bodies everywhere." She kneaded her hands, the memory of the battle tearing through her as though she were still there.

"Dead Scots or English?"

"Mostly English. Sir James only lost two men, with a few more injured. The English turned tail when Sir James struck down their leader. He told Maitland it was the toughest battle he'd ever fought."

Her grandmother reached out to take her hand. "But ye werenae hurt. And I'm sure ye fought hard."

"I struck many, just as ye taught me. But the aftermath, Grandmama. The screaming and the blood." She finally let a tear fall. "I dinnae wish to ever be in another battle like that again."

"How many?"

"They had four score, I think. We had half that, but we won."

Her grandmother broke into a deep, wet cough that kept her from answering.

"Oh, Grandmama. Ye arenae doing well at all, are ye?"

The woman known to strike fear in the hearts of men all across the land sighed and shook her head. "I fear this could be it, lass. I cannae fight this any longer. The pain is too much. My breathing is getting difficult." She coughed again.

"Nay." Eli shook her head so hard it hurt. "Nay. Just nay. I'll go speak with Aunt Brenna and I'll go get whatever potion or herb or weed or whatever she needs. Ye go back to sleep and I'll find a way to heal ye. I'm no' ready to lose ye. Not yet."

Her grandmother squeezed her hand and said, "Sometimes we have no choice."

"But I still do. There is much I can do and I will." She leaned over and gave her a kiss on her cheek. "Would ye like anything before I go?"

"Help me sip some broth, please?"

She helped her grandmother sit up. She wished she didn't have to because the movement pained her grandmother so much. Too much.

She had to speak with Aunt Brenna right away.

CHAPTER TWENTY-FIVE

ALARIC STOOD IN front of Logan and Gavin Ramsay in the courtyard that evening. "Gavin, I love yer daughter. We handfasted while we were on patrol. I know this is late, but I'd like yer blessing for our marriage. I hope to marry her properly someday soon."

"Why wait?" Logan asked. Eli's grandsire stood with his arms crossed.

Alaric had expected that question, and the answer was not negotiable. "I'd like my brother to be able to stand by my side. He is unable to do so at present."

"I hope he is well when ye return. Have ye discussed where ye will live? I'm happy to see another Grant marry a Ramsay, but there is always the choice of which clan to live with."

"Honestly we havenae discussed it. We have time. But when I go to visit my brother, I hope Eli will come along. I'd like her to meet my family. She knows some, but family is important to me."

"Ye have my approval. Welcome to our clan," Logan said, clasping his shoulder.

Gavin looked shocked. "Da, ye feeling all right?"

"Aye, why?"

"Ye never approve men for yer granddaughters that quickly. I welcome ye also, Alaric. Ye must be a rare man indeed if Eli agreed to handfast with ye. Treat my lassie well. I'll be watching, but I know yer clan has the same code as we do, so I trust ye will treat her well." Gavin motioned them all inside. "A wee celebration. I'll find the *breath of life* for all of us."

"And some for yer mother, Gavin. She needs more."

They stepped inside just as Eli came out of her grandmother's chamber. She made her way straight to Alaric and wrapped her arms around his waist, laying her head against his chest.

Eli's mother, Merewen, joined them. "I'm glad we have that settled at last. I spoke with Alaric while ye were in with yer grandmother, Eli. I like him. It was as if he was waiting for ye."

Alaric let out a breath and said, "I was. I think we will make a good life together, but I'm sorry things are troubled here. I know it was tough to see Gwyneth that sickly, Eli. I'm sorry."

"I still hope she can recover," Eli said, stepping back from Alaric's embrace. "Mama, I'm going to speak with Aunt Brenna. Alaric, come with me, please?"

He nodded and took her hand. "Where is she?"

Merewen embraced him as they began to move away from the group. "Welcome to the clan, Alaric. Eli, I'm happy for ye, though I wish ye'd shared with me sooner. A mother likes to hear these things directly from her daughter."

"Mama, I haven't had time. The battle was difficult and seeing Grandmama was worse." She paused and leaned her head on Alaric's chest again. "I didn't even know I liked him until this last patrol."

"Eli, were ye crying?" her sire asked, tipping his head to the side.

She nodded.

"We've no' seen that in a long time, Alaric," Merewen said. "But ye've had reason to. We have spoken with Aunt Brenna, and she is trying everything she can. We fear she's run out of ideas and treatments for Grandmama."

"I wish to speak with her myself."

"Go ther," Merewen said, waving them toward her chamber.

Alaric and Eli hurried across the great hall to the healing chamber. She opened the door and stuck her head around the corner looking for her aunt. "Aunt Brenna? May we come in? I would like to speak with ye about Grandmama."

"Come in, both of ye. And I hear ye have handfasted. Congratulations. Any Grant is welcome as a spouse here." She gave them both swift hugs before leading them to the small table in the center of the chamber. The walls were lined with pallets and cots. "I'm happy someone is keeping Quade's and my legacy going. A match between two powerful and wonderful clans. But I see the concern on yer face, Eli. Sit and we'll talk about Gwyneth."

Once they settled, Eli began questioning her aunt. "Is there no' something more ye can do for Grandmama?"

"I've tried everything. Nothing seems to be helping her at all. I've tried elderberry, wild sage, and chamomile. Jennie and I had made a nice mix of the three, and I've been using that. I dinnae know what else to do for her. Sometimes, there is nothing more I can do."

"What about Aunt Jennie? Can she no' come and try some of her treatments? Should I go ask her for help? There has to be something more we can do." Eli let go of Alaric's hand and was now rubbing her cheek so furiously that he thought she might tear the skin from her palms. He reached for her again and set her hand on his lap, using his thumb to draw circles in her palm in the hopes of calming her down.

Eli was a strong woman, but losing a grandparent was most difficult. When he'd lost his grandfather not long ago, he'd cried his heart out because it had hurt so much. He'd do anything to keep Eli from having to deal with loss just at this moment, on top of her first battle and their handfasting.

"Why do we no' go to visit Aunt Jennie to see if she's learned anything new," he suggested. "'Tis possible, is it no'? I've heard the monks receive news from traveling monks about treatments and new methods from Europe. True?"

Aunt Brenna's eyes lit up. "Aye. Aye. They do. In fact, 'tis where Aedan got her medicinal text long ago. They could have learned something new."

He looked to Eli for approval. "We could leave

at first light on the morrow. I'd like to visit Els within a sennight. We could stop along the way and see if Aunt Jennie has anything to help yer grandmother."

"And if she does?" Aunt Brenna asked.

"If so, we'll return. We can escort Aunt Jennie back or bring ye whatever herbs she thinks will help. Then we'll go to Grant land."

Eli threw her arms around Alaric with enough force that she nearly knocked him off the stool.

"Thank you, Alaric," she said into his ear. She turned back to the healer. "As much as I want to leave right now, I'm too tired to get back on a horse until morning. Is there a place where Alaric and I can sleep alone and no' be bothered? Can we sneak out the back and sleep in some cottage without Grandda noticing?"

"Lass, if ye handfasted with him, Logan willnae bother ye. He'll want ye to spend time alone."

Eli frowned and rubbed her cheek. "But in my chamber, I'll feel odd," she whispered. "And Ysenda is next door."

Aunt Brenna said, "Aye, I understand. I believe I have just the place for ye. Follow me. I'll tell any who asks that we are going for herbs, and I'll lead ye to a lovely cottage."

Aunt Brenna led the way, and to Alaric's surprise, no one questioned where they were headed, all too busy listening to Tevis's description of the Battle of Skaithmuir. He had to smile— he guessed he would be doing the same when he reached Grant land. Everyone loved hearing about battles.

When they stepped inside the cottage, Alaric waited to see what Eli thought of it. It didn't matter to him where they slept as long as she was in his arms. He had a strong need to be with her, to caress her, share thoughts on all that had happened.

He didn't want anyone's opinion but his wife's. His wife.

Eli said, "'Tis lovely, Aunt Brenna. Many thanks."

Aunt Brenna moved over to a cabinet and reached under the bottom shelf, pulling out a bottle of wine. "Raise a celebratory cup of this. I sleep out here on occasion in the warm months and keep it stocked with what I want. I have the place cleaned regularly. And there is always dried meat in the other cabinet. I can send a serving lass with something better, if ye like."

"Nay, please. We can find more on the morrow. I'm so tired that I feel like I will fall asleep standing up," Eli said, glancing at Alaric.

"If ye change yer mind, just send Alaric to the kitchens. On the morrow, come to the kitchen to find food for yer trip whenever ye are ready."

Eli gave her aunt a kiss and a hug, and Aunt Brenna left, closing the door softly behind her.

The moment they were alone, Eli grabbed Alaric, kissing him hard on the lips. He was happy to return it. They'd been too long unable to touch and caress each other. He teased her with his tongue, delving deep into her mouth, tasting all of her, and she followed his lead, doing whatever he did.

Even teasing his nipples. It didn't take long for him to respond to his wife, and her saucy smile let him know she'd noticed his erection.

"Ye like that ye have that power over me, do ye no', wife of mine?"

"I do, but I'll also apologize."

"Why?"

"Because I am exhausted. So if we dinnae hurry up, I'll fall asleep on ye for certes."

He scooped her up in his arms with a whoosh, swinging her wildly before depositing her on the bed. "Then we shallnae waste any time."

Alaric dropped his plaid to the floor and barely had the chance to remove his boots and trews before she reached for him, taking him in hand. "I missed ye."

He stayed her hand so he could help her out of her clothes and under the coverlet before he joined her in the bed. He had to admit she looked exhausted. "We can wait, Eli. We have many nights ahead of us."

She locked gazes with him and shook her head. "I need ye, Alaric. I need yer strength. I feel like I'm losing something powerful. I have to know I'll still have ye. Things have been too chaotic, too unpredictable."

He kissed her slowly, angling his mouth over hers, settling himself over her with his weight on his elbows. He kissed her lips, her neck, her ears, and trailed a path down her tender skin to the valley between her breasts, finally settling on her nipple. She arched her back and moaned, a sweet sound that went straight to his member.

"If ye moan like that much more, I'll lose my seed on yer leg and ye'll get naught."

She giggled and reached for him again, guiding him between her legs.

"Ye are ready for me? Are ye sure, lass?"

She nodded, that look she had about her telling him she was. And she was right. When he discovered how slick she was with her need, he entered her swiftly and only stopped when he was deep inside her. He whispered in her ear how much he loved her.

She whimpered and moved against him, pulling her knees up to take him deeper. Once she found her perfect position, placing him right where she wanted him, he thrust against her until they found their rhythm. They rocked together in sweet bliss until he reached down to bring her to finish quicker because he was so close.

As soon as she tightened around him, telling him she was climaxing, he went over the edge with a roar, and she shouted his name out, his orgasm bursting even more powerfully through him.

Hell, but they were great together. When they finished, he held still, enjoying being inside her for a wee bit more. When he began to shrink, he rolled off her and tucked her close.

He kissed her, but she didn't return the kiss.

Eli was fast asleep.

CHAPTER TWENTY-SIX

ELI GAVE HER horse a hug before she mounted, getting ready to leave for Cameron land. Their first true night together had been wonderful, though she'd been a bit embarrassed that she'd fallen asleep so quickly after their lovemaking.

Alaric approached her after filling a saddlebag with food. He whispered in her ear, "Are ye sure ye are no' sore this morn?"

"Nay. I'm fine. I just feel badly that I fell asleep so quickly."

"Ye more than made up for it in the middle of the night," he whispered before nibbling her ear. She squealed a wee bit, and he chuckled, his eyes sparkling.

This married life was quite nice.

They left Ramsay land and traveled with four guards, at her father's insistence. She didn't care—it was more important that they arrive on Cameron land safely. Surely Aunt Jennie would know of something that would kill the green discharge that continued to grow around her grandmother's knee. She didn't understand how they could wipe it all away and have it return the next day. And how did something in her knee give her a fever?

Where did it come from? What caused it? She had so many questions but Aunt Brenna was busy so she hated to bother her with them.

They rode with two guards leading and two guards behind them. The guards spoke amongst themselves, and there was some distance between them, so she felt safe asking Alaric a private question.

"Alaric, tell me more about ye and Uncle Jake. What truly happened? Why do ye consider it yer fault?"

Alaric closed his eyes, then glanced over at her. "I suppose I owe ye that much, sweeting." He stared up at the mostly gray sky, then sighed. "I have many uncles, and we all sparred at some point or another, and I often faced Uncle Jake. This particular day, the weather was a wee bit warm. We fought hard. I recall feeling the sweat drip down my back, and I saw it on my uncle's forehead. I think I was only twelve, and he is older than my sire, so he must have felt the heat more than I did."

Alaric rubbed his forehead, almost as if he were wiping away the same sweat from his memory. Perhaps Eli shouldn't have asked him about this. "Alaric, if ye wish to tell me later, 'tis fine."

"Nay, I'd prefer to finish now. I swung my sword from the side and knocked his weapon out of his hands. He crumpled to the ground and never came to again."

Eli thought hard about what he'd said. "Was he bleeding somewhere that ye never noticed while ye were fighting?"

"Nay. My sire checked him over. There was no blood anywhere. He died in seconds. My father said he was dead before he hit the ground."

"Did Aunt Brenna ever discern why he died? Was Aunt Jennie ever there to see him?"

"Aunt Jennie was there. She checked him over right away, and I recall her shaking her head. All she ever said was that it was his heart. But it was my fault. I pushed his heart too hard. Somehow, it had to be because of our sword fight. I feel like if I hadn't sparred with him, he might still be alive today. Poor Alasdair was so grief stricken, especially after losing his mother less than a year before. Alasdair refused to even discuss what happened. None of us could talk about it for a long time because Alasdair couldn't bear it."

"Still?"

"Och, nay. Dyna scared it out of him a year later. He just had too much loss too quickly. And he has no siblings. Probably why he and Emmalin had two children right away. He resents that he had no siblings like the rest of us have. Odd that it worked out that way."

"But I still think ye are wrong. If he had no' died that day, what about the next day? If his heart was bad, would it no' have happened the next day or the next moon? I dinnae see how ye believe it to be yer fault."

Alaric sighed, then said, "I thank ye for that. Many have told me the same. I guess because I was so young that it left such an impression on me. I'd dealt with death before, but never right in front of me. I surely have seen more of it on the battlefield now."

"It had to have been a shocking experience. I understand that."

"It was." His gaze drifted off into the distance.

Eli hoped the memory might begin to disappear now. She hoped to fill his mind with more pleasant events, but before she could suggest it, she was cut short. A group of riders approached, and Eli was pleased to see that it was Brin with a few guards.

"Greetings, Brin! How is Ceit? I cannae wait to see her." She'd always loved Ceit, and she hadn't seen her in a while.

"She's hale and she'll be excited to see ye both," Brin replied. "Ye will stay the night, at least? Ye are headed to Grant land?"

"Aye. One or two nights. Then we'll move on." Eli glanced at Alaric to see his thoughts, and he nodded his agreement.

"Wonderful. We just finished our meal and we have plenty left. Enough for ye and yer guards."

Later that night, she and Alaric sat around the hearth with Aunt Jennie, Brin, and Ceit. They told them about the battle they'd endured and answered all their questions, while Eli grew more impatient with every passing moment. She had burning questions to ask.

Finally, she couldn't wait any longer. "Yer pardon, but may I ask ye a healing question, Aunt Jennie? Grandmama has taken verra ill. Aunt

Brenna has tried all her potions and ointments on her, and naught is working."

"What kind of sickness is it?" Aunt Jennie asked. "Or is it still her knee?"

"She hurt her knee, turned it when she stepped in a hole. The next morning, it had swelled up, and now she has that green stuff leaking on the bandages, and she has a fever that Aunt Brenna cannae stop. Have ye any ideas? Or have ye heard of anything new from the monks?"

"Nay, I know of nothing new. My apologies to ye. Gwyneth has had trouble with her knee for a long time. It is indeed persistent."

The door opened and Uncle Aedan stuck his head inside. "Brin, could ye join me outside, please? Ceit, ye can come along too, if ye like."

The two left and Aunt Jennie said to Eli, "I could visit Gwyneth after I check on Maeve's bairn. I was told Maitland was on his way, so I'd like to be here when they arrive. She has requested me or my sister to help her deliver."

"Maitland told us he would be coming. When is Maeve's time, Auntie?" Eli asked.

"She is not due to have her bairn for at least two or three moons, I believe. I'm no' sure why they are coming so soon, but they are welcome. But if I see all is well with Maeve and I get her settled here, I can visit Gwyneth quickly, then return. Would that make ye feel better, Eli?"

All she could do was nod. Her voice caught in her throat. She didn't like the possibility that there was nothing they could do for her grandmother. Perhaps they could head straight to Grant land.

They had healers like everyone else did. Could they have a suggestion? Or what if they traveled to Inverness? Would a healer there have an idea Aunt Brenna did not have?

Anxious, she reached for Alaric's hand and squeezed it. Alaric kissed the back of her hand, and warmth rushed through her, the warmth that she attributed to knowing that he loved her, that he would always protect her, and that he would always be there for her.

Eli immediately thought of Alaric's Uncle Jake. Speaking her mind as she often did, she said, "I dinnae know which is worse—lingering like Grandmama or dying in a heartbeat like Jake did."

"Alaric," Aunt Jennie said, tilting her head in that pensive way she had. "Funny Eli mentions that, I was thinking about ye and yer uncle the other day. Ye dinnae still have any of those strange beliefs about Jake's death, do ye?"

Eli's gaze shot to Alaric's.

"Aunt Jennie, I know I had a hand in his death, and…"

Jennie's hand reached for his. "Stop, please, Alaric. Ye had naught to do with his death."

Alaric searched her face and asked, "Are ye certain of that? Because I was the one who struck him before he died. Just moments before he took his last breath." His voice caught, and Eli had the distinct impression he was about to shed a few tears.

"As I explained to my brother, Jake had a hidden illness. I recall when he was young and he complained he couldn't breathe for no obvious reason, so I listened to his heart. His beats were different than everyone else's beats. His heartbeat did not have a regular pattern like it is supposed to. It would skip or go too fast. I checked him the next time I saw him, and it was normal. A steady strong beat, no odd pattern to it. And he didn't have trouble with his breathing until many years later."

Aunt Jennie chewed on her bottom lip and stared off into space. "I asked another healer about this once when I was in Edinburgh, and they spoke of an enlarged heart. That sometimes they would be fine, and other times not. That they would have a difficult time breathing one day, and the next day they would be fine. I asked them if a large heart could kill someone, and he said it was possible that it shortened one's life. He'd never seen such a malady in anyone older. He assumed that meant they would die young."

"I have never heard of such an ailment," Eli said.

"'Twas my first experience with it, but I believe that is what happened to Jake. But if his heart was enlarged, his death would be attributed to his overexertion, not in anything ye did. And it might just have been his time. He'd had many harder bouts than sparring with a lad just learning to swing a sword."

"But I hit him, and he died."

"Nay, he swung more than a score of times, and he couldn't swing again. 'Tis how I see it. His heart gave out before yer sword met his on that last swing. He lifted his sword and his heart denied him. 'Twas why he lost his grip on his sword. I'd be more likely to blame it on my brother's blood that was in him, that ferocity that would no' quit for any reason. Alex was quite competitive, and so are all his lads. Jake overworked his heart, no' ye, Alaric. His body must have told him to quit, but he didn't."

Alaric glanced from Aunt Jennie to Eli and then back again. "Do ye believe that to be true, Auntie?"

"Aye. His death had naught to do with ye, Alaric. Ye were young. Please dinnae think on it again." She patted his shoulder and got up to go to the sideboard.

Eli reached for his hand and squeezed it, his face clearly showing relief. How happy she was for him.

The door opened and Uncle Aedan entered with a stranger, and their conversation fell silent.

"Jennie, this is Egan. He came looking for Maitland, so I told him he could sleep in the guards' quarters until Maitland arrives. Do ye have a meat pie for him? The guards have ale enough, but they finished their meal."

"Aye, there are two pies sitting on the sideboard, Aedan. I'll get him one."

Alaric rose and approached the stranger. Alaric seemed tense to Eli, and she wondered what he was thinking.

"What do ye want with Maitland?"

Eli held her breath, waiting to see what the stranger would answer.

Alaric went on when the man didn't answer.

"Are ye English? Ye look familiar to me. Were ye no' at the battle near Skaithmuir?"

Everyone in the hall froze.

CHAPTER TWENTY-SEVEN

A LARIC COULD HAVE sworn he'd seen this man before, and recently. It had to be in Skaithmuir. He took a step closer to him.

"English?" Egan looked aghast at Alaric's words. "Nay, but I did fight with Sir James. I'm a Scot, born and bred."

"So why do ye seek Maitland?"

"I wish to travel with his patrol. I live too far north to keep traveling to the Borderlands to fight and earn coin. Once I see Maitland, I'm sure he'll accept me on his patrol. I prefer to fight in the Highlands. I'm happy to sleep with the guards. I'll not be bothering the chieftain's family. Ye have my word on that."

The man had short brown hair and a full beard. Nothing unusual there. His skin carried the color of the sun as if he worked outdoors. But there was something in his eyes that Alaric didn't like.

As long as he stayed outside, far from Eli, he wouldn't bother him. His sudden need to protect her and keep her hidden from this man overpowered him.

The bastard would not touch Eli.

The man took his meat pies, thanked the Camerons, then left the hall. Alaric looked to Eli for confirmation of what he thought.

"Was he familiar to ye?"

She stared after the man for a moment. "I think so."

"English?"

"Nay. I think he was Scottish. I think he was among the guards of Sir James."

"He better be Scottish. I'll find out if he's no'."

Eli moved closer and rested her hand on his forearm. "Alaric, dinnae worry. We need no' worry about that man. He's gone."

"Fine. I'll be fine. I'll chat with Brin." He moved over closer to Ceit and Brin, sitting in a different chair while Eli chatted with Aunt Jennie.

He had to admit that the last conversation he'd had with his aunt had opened his eyes. It was as if a giant weight had lifted off his shoulders. When Aunt Jennie had assured him that he had not been the cause of Uncle Jake's death, Alaric had felt so incredibly grateful that he didn't know what to say.

Jake's death had been caused by his heart giving up, not from a blow that Alaric had delivered. Jennie was right of course—the chance of a twelve-year-old hitting a man with the flat of his sword hard enough to kill him was tiny, even smaller when the man was the son of Alex Grant. The knowledge meant everything to Alaric.

He had not killed his uncle.

Which meant that he probably hadn't hurt Alasdair either. He had to hope that Alasdair did not suffer from the same affliction.

The door opened and Uncle Aedan entered, moving over to sit next to him. "Everything well out there, Uncle?"

The old chieftain thought for a moment, then said, "I cannae say why, but I dinnae trust that man, Egan. Do ye know aught of him? Was he at the battle?"

Alaric rubbed his hands together, something he did to keep himself from grabbing for his weapon, though he did not have it near to hand at the moment. "Both Eli and I believe we recognize him from the battle. Eli is quite confident he was a Scot. I wasn't sure, but I trust her memory. What makes you uneasy?"

"When I left him with the other guards, I made a point of circling back around outside the building to listen to their conversation. I do the same with every stranger who stops here, just to be careful. He was asking about the archers. He was shocked that there were such skilled female archers. He asked who trained them and how many there were. But the comment he made that I truly didnae like was when he mentioned he was looking for a wife and asked if the archers were married or not. Said he saw four of them on the battlefield. Correct?"

"Aye," Alaric answered, trying to remain calm while he settled his thoughts. "Dyna, Eli, Thea, and Wenna. Was he interested in any one archer in particular?"

If Egan had mentioned Eli's name, Alaric was about to beat someone to the size of a hazelnut.

"He wishes to marry a dark-haired lass." Aedan gave him that look that told him all he needed to know.

He bolted out of his chair and headed out the door, calling out behind him, "I'll return in a moment, wife. Please dinnae follow me."

He knew she would anyway, but he hoped not for a few moments. He headed toward the guards' quarters, opened the door and bellowed, "Come on out here, ye scab-faced pustule. Or are ye spineless too?"

The talk amongst the guards fell silent, and the men looked at each other in puzzlement. Then Egan got up and strode forward, his innocent expression becoming a smug, aggressive look as fast as a bolt of lightning.

"Who are ye calling scab-faced?"

"Whoever the bastard is who wants to marry my wife. Is that no' ye?"

"Are ye married to one of the dark-haired lasses? Because I dinnae want that white-haired one. She's too old. And the other one is too wide in the hip. I like my women thin. So I'll take either of the other two. And I'd like to test one out this eve if I may. Which one are ye giving me?" The man had the bollocks to stride right up to him, his face less than a hand's length from Alaric.

And Alaric couldn't resist the temptation of shutting the arrogant bastard up. He put his fist in his face, then lifted him up and tossed him across the floor. "Ye want more, then get up and come back, ye weasel."

He'd heard a decisive crack when his fist had connected with the man's nose, so he wasn't surprised to see blood pouring out.

The fool held his hand up and said, "I'll no' be bothering them. Ye go on yer way. I'll wait here for Menzie."

He had no doubt that he would wait for Maitland, but first he had to speak with Uncle Aedan and advise him of exactly what the man had said. He could go after Wenna, after all, and he didn't think Tevis would approve.

The door opened and Eli stepped inside. He glanced over his shoulder, but waited to make sure Egan was not going to try a move toward her before he went to her.

"Stay the hell away," he snarled.

He turned around and set his hand on Eli's waist, though he wished to hug her tight to let the fool know who she belonged to and who she preferred. But he knew she would be confused, so he led her outside before speaking to her.

Brin was just outside the door, about to come in. "Everything well?"

Alaric rubbed his skinned knuckles. "All is well now. The fool thought he could marry one of our archers. One of the dark-haired ones."

Eli's head snapped toward him at his words, and he ran his hand through her dark, silky strands. "I let him know ye werenae available. He's convinced."

He glanced over his shoulder as the door

opened and Egan stepped outside, still trying to stop the blood from pouring out of his nose.

He glared at Alaric, who stepped in front of Eli. "Dinnae even look at her."

Egan looked at Alaric, pointed his finger, and said, "This is not over."

"Aye, it is. Leave now." Alaric was confident Aedan would agree with him, and he hoped Brin would back him up as well.

Brin nodded. "Take yer horse and get off Cameron land. I'll have ye escorted."

Egan left, but not without glancing back one more time at Eli.

The bastard winked at her.

Alaric would have followed the fool, just to make sure he was truly leaving, but Brin said, "Let him go."

Eli squeezed his hand and said, "Please leave him for now. Ye let him know how ye feel already. I can tell by yer bloody knuckles."

Somehow, Alaric knew he'd be seeing Egan again.

CHAPTER TWENTY-EIGHT

E LI RODE NEXT to Alaric two days later, nearly on Grant land. She'd spent much of her time on Cameron land with Jennie, anxious to learn anything she could from the wise healer. Unfortunately, she didn't know much more about her grandmother's affliction than Aunt Brenna did. The longer she was away from the woman, the more she worried.

Alaric had busied himself in the lists when he hadn't been patrolling the land for the skunk named Egan, but no one had seen any evidence of the fool since the first night.

Eli had to admit she was getting anxious to return to her grandmother to check on how she was doing. Worried that she was going to lose her, this next journey could take her two ways. One was to talk with Gracie, the primary healer on Grant land, about Grandmama's affliction.

Her second thought, more of a fear, was whether she would return to Ramsay land too late, if she rode from healer to healer looking for answers.

Alaric held her hand, riding abreast of her, as they approached. "Sweeting, ye are thoughtful.

Ye arenae worried about the visit, are ye?" He glanced over at her, and the look on his face swelled her heart a bit.

He did love her, and even more frightening was that she loved him. A part of her didn't wish to be attached to anyone because that meant she could lose him. The fear of losing her grandmother was crossing into every part of her life.

"I'm just worried about Grandmama."

"I understand. Ye will chat with my mother about sickness?"

"Aye," she replied, not willing to admit that she'd nearly lost hope.

"I know that Aunt Jennie and Aunt Brenna are the most renowned, but it cannae hurt to talk to every healer ye meet, aye?'

"Agreed." She took a deep breath. She was also a wee bit nervous about meeting Alaric's parents. She'd met them before when she'd been here for summer festivals, but this was different. He was introducing her as his wife.

She wasn't given much time to think about it. The bellows of the Grant war whoop reached her ears, startling her, and the thundering of hoofbeats convinced her they were nearly there.

The look on Alaric's face told her he was glad to be home. She couldn't help but wonder where they would live—Grant land or Ramsay land? She wasn't given much time to consider her quandary before a sea of red plaids on horseback surrounded them, the riders hooting loud enough to scare the birds out of the trees.

"Elshander? Is that ye?" Alaric called out. "Ye are back to yer usual state?"

Their younger brother, Jowell, called out, "He rides better than he walks, Alaric, but he's working on it."

Alaric's smile lit up Eli's entire being. He'd dropped her hand and grabbed both reins. "Can ye race me, Els?" He glanced over to her, and she waved him on.

Lads loved to compete, no matter how old they were. She watched as Els yelled out to him as he spun his horse, and the two raced toward the castle.

Eli gasped. It had been a while since she'd visited Grant Castle, and the size of it always astounded her. They had the most towers of any castle she'd ever seen. Her gaze took in all the beauty of the Highlands around the castle.

A small village sat in front of the curtain wall, with fields being readied for planting spreading around it. To the far side of the castle were the beautiful hills of the Highlands, rocky in spots but lush in other small areas with the promise of impending summer. In the distance, the mountains looked as though the peaks nearly touched the clouds. A loch sat on the far side of the village, beyond a large orchard of apple and pear trees.

The loch reminded her of the memories she loved most. The two clans alternated their summer festival, entertaining each other with feasting, competitions, and entertainment. Her favorite had always been the swimming competitions in the loch. This loch was larger than the Ramsay loch, and it had several cottages on the far side of it.

She'd caught her first fish off one of the two docks on this loch. And she'd dared to go on the contraption Alex had built, with the help of his armorer, on the end, one they could slide on with a burlap bag. It sat partway up the hill and once on it, the slippery surface would take you directly into the water.

She recalled staring at it in awe, and Uncle Quade had strode up to Alex and said, "Ye just had to try and outdo me, did ye no', Grant?"

Alex had laughed and clasped his shoulder. "And I did, did I no'?"

Uncle Quade had narrowed his gaze and said, "Mayhap for this year. Wait until ye see what I have next year."

And the competition carried on. She'd loved sliding down that contraption, landing with a big splash at the end. She and her cousins ate fruit tarts and pastries until their bellies ached, and they'd competed in multiple archery tournaments every year.

It just hit her that she was now a true member of Clan Grant, and that thought brought tears to her eyes. She loved the Grants with all her heart, and she adored the man who was shouting and laughing with his brothers as they approached the castle gates. She was in awe of how much her life had changed in such a short time.

Once they arrived at the castle, Alaric helped her dismount, something she swore she'd never allow, but she found out she rather liked her husband's hands at her waist, giving them the opportunity for a wee bit of intimacy when others were around. Once they stepped away from the stable lads, Alaric tugged her close as he approached his two brothers, his father seated in a large chair in the courtyard a short distance away. He waited until he was close to his sire, his brothers following. "Meet my wife, Eli. We handfasted while on patrol."

Els looked at her and asked, "Are... ye... sick, lass?" His words came out slower than usual, but he had a big smile on his face.

She shook her head and laughed.

Jowell picked up the joke. "She had to be ill to agree to marry ye, Alaric."

His father said, "Welcome to Clan Grant as a Grant this time, lass. We are pleased to have ye as a true part of the family. Lads, help me inside. Yer mother will wish to know this news right away." Jowell and Els lifted him, getting Jamie settled in Els's arms so he could carry him inside, Jowell guarding the still splinted leg.

The laughter and teasing continued, but Alaric set his hand at the small of her back and ushered her inside, introducing her to everyone as his wife.

His mother rushed down the steps from the balcony toward them, her eyes widening when she saw that he had his hand at her waist.

"We have news, Mama," Alaric said. "Eli and I handfasted."

"A Ramsay-Grant wedding! I love it!" She

hugged Eli, then her son, tears misting her gaze. Gracie looked frazzled, but even so, she was lovely. Eli recalled hearing that Gracie had been considered one of the loveliest lasses in the Highlands, and she was still beautiful.

It was a chaotic but happy arrival, but it didn't take long before Eli was suddenly overcome by exhaustion. They'd been on the road for most of the day. She leaned over to whisper in his ear, "Alaric, I think I need to rest."

His mother must have heard her because she bolted up from her chair and said, "Alaric, the poor lass is exhausted. Allow me to show her to yer new chamber."

"A new chamber?" Alaric asked in surprise.

"Aye, ye arenae sleeping in the same chamber as yer brother. Ye may have the guest chamber. 'Tis always at the ready so it will fit ye perfectly. Eli deserves a lovely chamber for her first night here as a Grant."

"Do ye mind going with her, or would ye rather I take ye?" Alaric whispered in her ear.

"I have questions for your mother, so stay with yer brothers." She knew he had much to say to Els, so she gave him a push.

"Come," Gracie said, motioning for Eli to follow her up the stairs. "Ye have surprised me, but I'm pleased with Alaric's choice. How is yer family, Eli?"

"Mama and Papa are fine, but Grandmama is not doing well."

Gracie gave her a questioning look as they walked down the passageway and into a chamber at the end. "This chamber has a lovely view of the mountains when ye pull the fur back. We are getting shutters made for our windows, but we havenae installed them all yet. The lads will bring yer saddlebag up for ye, and I'll send an ewer of fresh water so ye may wash up. I'll send some dried fruit and an apple along also. Is there anything else I can get for ye?"

"Nay, but may I ask ye a question or two, if ye please?"

"Of course." There were two chairs in front of the hearth. Gracie sat in one and motioned for her to sit in the other. "Ask whatever ye wish."

Eli explained the situation with her grandmother's knee and told her what she knew of Aunt Brenna's treatments thus far. "Naught is working. Have ye any suggestions on what else could be done?"

Gracie thought for a moment, then said, "Ye came from Cameron land? Did ye ask Jennie?"

"I did. She didnae have any suggestions."

"Hmmm. Allow me to think on it a bit, and I'll confer with Caralyn, but I doubt we have anything that Aunt Brenna and Aunt Jennie would not have suggested. We both learned all our skills from them."

"Is there another healer in the area that ye are familiar with?"

"Nay, we are the only healers around. The closest ones to Inverness are Brigid, Tara, and Jennet, but ye know they were trained the same as we were. Ye have already consulted with the best in the land. I am sorry they couldnae offer any help."

"I feared ye would say that."

Gracie patted her hand and said, "I've found that sometimes the patient has to make the decision to heal. We cannae help everyone, I'm sorry to tell ye. I wish we could. But if Aunt Brenna cannae help Gwyneth, I dinnae know of anyone else to refer ye to. I'm so sorry."

"Dinnae be. I expected yer answer. I know how special Aunt Brenna and Aunt Jennie are."

"And sometimes, all of a sudden someone heals and we cannae explain it. Ye could go home and find yer grandmother all better. Sometimes, people heal themselves. 'Tis rare, though."

She had to pray that would be the case. Otherwise, the situation for her dear grandmother was hopeless.

Gracie stood and headed toward the chamber door, then she paused. "Lass, would ye like to soak in the tub? I just had one filled for myself, but I would like to visit with Alaric first. Would ye like to make use of the warm water? Ye recall Maddie's bathing room? The tub is full, the towels and the oils are all ready for ye. And ye will find a dressing gown for when ye are ready to return to yer room."

Eli's eyes widened at the thought. "I would love that. 'Tis at the other end of the passageway, correct?"

"Aye. Ye enjoy it and everything ye need will be in yer chamber when ye are finished." Gracie patted her hand, and Eli nearly ran down the passageway.

She stripped out of her clothing quickly, set a toe into the steaming liquid, then sighed, sinking into the heat slowly to savor the pleasure. Living on Grant land definitely had some benefits, and this fine bathing chamber was one of them.

Settling back in the tub so her entire body was covered, she closed her eyes and smiled, thinking of all that had taken place. Ignoring the worst, her grandmother's health, there had been much good in her life. She'd participated in a successful battle and survived, her sister was hale and happy, and she'd become closer to many of her cousins like Thea and Wenna.

And then there was Alaric. How had she never truly noticed him before?

She hadn't been looking for a man, of course. Even deliberately *not* looking. Sometimes her stubbornness did her more harm than good, perhaps. Reyna had been absolutely correct. She'd had no idea that coupling with a man would be so pleasurable. The first night had been good, besides the brief pain, but their night together in Aunt Brenna's cottage had been so wonderful. Who knew you could do it that often?

And last eve on Cameron land? She'd admitted to being sore, between the horse and their activities, so Alaric had just held her, and she'd been so warm she fell asleep instantly. Married life had some benefits, and she had a feeling she was just beginning to learn about Alaric Grant.

Once the water cooled, she stepped out, loving

the smell and the feel of the lavender oil on her skin. She rubbed her skin dry then wrapped a dressing gown around her body and the towel around her hair. She had to admit that this towel was thicker and bigger than any she had in her home. Someday she'd ask Gracie who made them; she'd love one of her own. She gathered up her clothes and left the warm chamber.

In the passageway, she overheard the men all laughing and chatting in the hall. She stopped at the balcony, leaned over, and the noise instantly quieted as the group all turned to stare up at her.

"Alaric, I'm going to bed. Come whenever."

Alaric's expression was one of shock. "What are ye wearing?"

"A dressing gown. I just got out of the bathing tub."

"The bathing tub? Ye had hot water?"

"I did and it was heavenly. 'Tis still a wee bit warm if ye'd like to wash up a wee bit." Then she leaned over, and once she realized his mother and father were no longer there, gave him that look of desire that would rile him for sure.

She headed down the passageway, breaking into giggles when Alaric said, "See ye all on the morrow."

More hoots and hollers and laughter followed. She stepped into the bedchamber, almost closing the door, but he opened it behind her. "I'll be right back, Eli. I'm going to wash up. Promise not to fall asleep?"

She dropped the dressing gown and said, "I'll be waiting for ye."

He left the chamber so fast that she laughed. Gracie had left a beautiful night rail on the bed, so she donned that, moving over to sit in front of the fire while she brushed her hair.

The door opened a few moments later and she stood, turning to look at her husband. He entered and dropped his towel.

She wished she could whistle but she didn't have that skill. "Ye look so clean."

She took two steps, but he held his hand up. "Stop, please."

Casting a puzzled gaze his way, she waited to see what his issue was.

"Lassie mine, ye are so beautiful. I can see through that gown and yer profile is so…"

She didn't give him the chance to finish, instead making her way over and slowly tossing her gown onto a chair. "I'm here and I'm ready for ye."

She stood on her tiptoes and kissed him, devouring him, the taste of ale fresh on his lips. She teased him with her tongue just long enough until he swept her up in his arms and pulled the coverlet back to deposit her in the bed.

"Ye smell of lavender," he said. "Everywhere?"

Flat on her back, she stared up at the ceiling while her husband kissed every part of her body, letting her know which spots were the most fragrant.

But when his lips landed *there*…she pushed up on her elbows and said, "What the hell are ye doing?"

He lifted his head and said, "Tasting ye. Why do ye no' lie back and see if ye like it?"

Still scowling, she did as he asked.

"Alaric!" How the hell could something like that feel so good? She had wished to tell him to stop because it was so odd, but now she only had one thought. Hell, nay! *Keep going.*

She wriggled and writhed, finally grabbing his hair to keep him exactly where she wanted, fighting to keep her moans quiet. This was something meant to be private. Of that much she was certain.

She nearly crossed the chasm into her orgasm, but he lifted his head and said, "Eli? Will ye let go of my hair?"

Her hands flew away. What the hell should she do with them now? They landed on her breasts, and she pinched her nipples without thinking. Alaric's eyes widened.

"'Tis enough for now. I need ye, lass."

He entered her quickly, their moans mingling together. She lifted her legs and wrapped them around him, and he thrust into her, plunging so deep that she moaned again, this time a wee bit too loud.

Then she crashed over the precipice, calling out to her husband as he finished with a roar.

Marriage was fun.

CHAPTER TWENTY-NINE

ELI COULD BARELY wait to get back to Ramsay land. She'd been so excited when they'd reached the tree that signaled the crossover that she nearly hooted.

And Alaric noticed.

"Ye are that excited to be home again?"

"God's b..." Hell, but she knew Alaric hated when she cursed about the Lord so she changed it for him. "Spit and slime, but aye, I'm glad. I'm so worried about Grandmama. Forgive me, but I fear she may no' still be alive."

He grabbed the reins of her horse to pull her closer, then leaned over and kissed her neck. She couldn't stop the quick reaction she had to the brawny man, her insides twittering as she gasped with delight. Aye, but she did enjoy the physical part of their relationship.

"I thank ye for changing yer words," he said.

"What words did I change?" Dammit to hell, but he made her forget everything.

"God's?"

"Och, aye, ye are correct. I did it to please ye, so I'm happy ye noticed." She was gloriously glad no one could see them when he stuck his tongue out and wagged it at her with a saucy grin. She blushed so quickly that he broke out in guffaws.

Hell, but she'd not forgotten how he'd used that tongue of his. Her mind couldn't help but go to that activity, and she wondered if she could return the favor. She glanced over at him, her tongue licking her lips and his reaction was instantaneous.

"Dinnae do that. And whatever ye are thinking, please dinnae say it. Please!"

She threw her head back and laughed, pleased she had thought of something new for them to try.

A few moments later, her sire and brother were nearly upon them. Kyle and Kyler with them.

"Ye had a safe journey? No English roaming about after Skaithmuir?" her father asked.

"No one bothered us," Alaric replied. "Though we did meet a fool of a Scot on Cameron land. Brin sent him out, and we've not seen him since. I wouldnae be surprised if he turns up, though."

Eli had to agree with Alaric about Egan. She didn't think he was done bothering them.

Alaric went on. "Ye havenae met a Scot named Egan here, have ye? He was looking for an archer to marry. Thought he'd grab Eli."

Her father's eyes widened. "What happened?"

"Ye need no' worry. My fist in his face convinced him she was unavailable."

Her father grinned and said, "Nice job, Grant."

Eli rolled her eyes at the story. The foolish bastard had thought he could just walk up and take her simply because he wanted her. As if no lass had the right to make her own decision over who she married.

"Daughter? Ye are hale? Ye look a wee bit grumpy."

"I'm fine, Da. I was just thinking of that fool thinking he could just take me and I'd have to marry him. I wish he had tried. I would have kicked him in the bollocks until he cried."

"Good thing Mama isn't here to hear ye talk like that, Eli." Her brother's taunt came out in a singing tone.

"Close yer mouth, Errol." She glared at her brother, and they all laughed.

Of course they would laugh. None of them knew what it was like to be a lass and have everyone else make your decisions for you. Or try to. "Da, how is Grandmama?"

"No improvement, lass. I'm worried, and so is Grandda."

"May I go see her?"

"Aye. Grandda is in the stables brushing down his horse. She's sitting and watching the archers practice. Go visit with her. She'll appreciate it."

"She's outside?"

"Aye, Grandda brought her out because she's miserable inside. And 'tis a pretty spring day. There are clouds but ye can see the blue sky and the air is warm. Even the birds seem happy today."

They came up to the archery field and her sire pointed her grandmother out. "She's just there. Go visit her, and we'll be in the hall. Alaric, come with us. I wish to hear more about this Egan."

Eli said, "Then I definitely will visit her, because I dinnae wish to hear anything more about that arsehole."

Her father shook his head slowly. "Alaric, it doesnae bother ye, her cursing? Her mother always gets after her."

"She gave up blaspheming for me. I can't ask more than that, Gavin."

Her father laughed, and they went their separate ways, parting with a wave. She drew up close, pleased to see her grandmother was awake in her chair, her bad leg propped up on a cushioned stool. She was engrossed in watching Ysenda, Thea, Willum, Wenna, and a few others practice. Eli tethered her horse and joined her grandmother, sitting in the grass next to her.

"Greetings, Grandmama. I see Grandda found ye a nice chair."

"Och, he did. My back hurts too much to sit in the grass, and I'd never get up again. This is perfect for me."

"What is it made of?"

"Donnan made it for me. Bethia sewed the cloth around the wood so I can settle in it with my back up. All I need is a stump to rest my foot on, and I'm all set. Now I can come out here every day if the weather is fine."

"How is yer knee? And yer fever?"

"No better. Aunt Brenna says she cannae do anything more for me."

"Then ye can fight it on yer own. Ye might still get better."

"Nay, lass. If I were yer age, I might, but no'

being the old lady I am. I know no' how much longer, but I think I may only see one more Christmas."

Eli grabbed on to that thought. One Christmas. She wouldn't have guessed she could hold on that long, so that certainly eased her worries. And perhaps by then, they would discover something new to help her.

"How was yer trip with yer new husband? The Grants were happy to see ye? And how are Alaric's brother and father?"

"We had a nice trip to see his family. His father still canno' walk and has to protect his leg with that splint, but his sons move him about. And Els was on his horse. He struggles to walk fast, but he is moving on his own. He talks, but slowly, and the bump on his head is nearly gone. Alaric was pleased to see his progress."

"And they accepted ye as Alaric's wife?"

"Aye. Did ye think they wouldnae?"

"Nay, I knew they would. Yer sister is making big plans. Ye might wish to go ask her about them."

Her sister must have heard her grandmother because she squealed and raced back to give Eli a big hug. "Guess what? We're planning a wedding."

"Ye are? I thought ye handfasted."

"We did, but now we wish for a big wedding. And Tevis is marrying Wenna, and Thea and Willum said they would marry along with us."

"All of ye together?"

"Aye, Lily said it would be so much fun, and I agree. Ye will join us?"

Eli kind of liked the idea. She hadn't asked Alaric about a formal wedding, but why not?

"I wish Rab was still here to marry ye, but his friend is," her grandmother said.

"I'll ask Alaric. But when will it be? He probably would want his parents and his siblings here."

"In about a fortnight, I think. They could get here by then. We already sent word to Black Isle, so I'm hoping some of them will come. The messenger will stop on Grant land on the way back. Say ye'll join yer wedding with ours."

"Alaric and I haven't talked about a wedding. But I'll think on it and see what he says."

"Good enough for now. I'm going to practice a bit more. Join us?" Ysenda asked.

"Nay, I'll stay with Grandmama." She didn't say it, but she wondered if Aunt Brigid knew how sickly her mother was. If the crew came from Black Isle, that would mean they'd have three more healers here to look at Grandmama's leg.

"Ye'd rather be here with an old woman than yer sister?" Her grandmother gave her a pointed look.

"Right now, I would. Besides, I have a question for ye. I wish to hear yer thoughts."

"I'm listening, lass."

"Alaric's family want him to be laird."

She watched her grandmother carefully, not surprised to see her brows arch in surprise, but then she tipped her head to one side. "Did he tell ye why?"

"Aunt Jennie doesnae think Els will be ready to be laird for some time. And Jamie is getting on in years. With his leg, he suggested Alaric should replace him."

"And what does Alaric say? And did Els agree?"

"Els did agree, and Alaric said he needed to think on it. They want an answer in a moon."

"And how do ye feel about being a laird's wife?"

Eli tucked her legs in so she could rest her elbows on her knees. "I'm no' sure. I think I would be all right after a while, but I am young. Gracie said she would help us, of course. And so did Jamie. And Connor, of course, will still be leading as well."

"Quade believed in passing the lairdship along so he could help Torrian. He didn't want to wait until he died. Said it would be too much pressure on Torrian. I think he's right."

"I love the Grants and the castle, but I would have to live there, not here. That troubles me."

"Ye could visit whenever ye wish."

"True, but what does a laird's wife do?"

"It doesn't take special training. It takes a special constitution, a good mind, and a big heart. Ye have all three." Her grandmother smiled at her, and Eli took her hand.

"I'm no' special."

"Ye recall the sapphire sword, lass?"

"Of course. The one John holds."

"Well, they say there is a special medal that is given to a certain lass, like the sword is given to a warrior."

"I've never heard about it."

"The faeries in the land of the Scots decide

which lass has the talent to be a leader of several clans. 'Tis a legend."

"Has any lass ever been given it?"

"None that I know of. But since it's a legend, I thought I would pass it on. Because even the faeries know that women have good minds, like Avelina Menzie, and that they can lead alongside men. Some think women would make better leaders."

"Why have I never heard of this medal?"

"Because no one has seen it. Someone suggested that the woman who holds it keeps it hidden, so greedy men won't steal it. I dinnae know who saw it last, but 'tis still a legend, so we must pass the tale on. 'Tis our duty to our ancestors and to those who come after us."

"I wonder if it will be passed on in my lifetime. Tell me more about it."

"I think it takes a special person to be able to see what a land can become instead of what a land was in the past. And if it is a lass who has it, she must be special because she has to be able to stand up to men. Avelina did, but now the sword has passed on to a male, young John. It's time for the medal to be found, and 'twill be a lass who finds it."

"Found?"

"Whoever finds the medal is the one chosen by the faeries. They leave it where they know she will find it. The faeries see all and know all. Never forget that."

CHAPTER THIRTY

SEVERAL DAYS LATER, Alaric came in from the lists, wiping the sweat from his brow. He enjoyed sparring with different people, especially the Ramsays. Torrian's son Lachlan was quite powerful, and so were Cadyn and Cailean. He headed to the sideboard to grab an ale, glancing over at the group of lasses studying something over a trestle table.

Eli had approached him about getting married as part of the group wedding, and he'd agreed. He'd been surprised it had come from her, but she wished to marry with the others. The more time he spent with the wee siren, the more he wanted her. This way he'd never have to worry about the year and a day shite. She'd not be leaving him in a year. Or ever. There was a large crowd of Grants on their way, along with many others—Mathesons, Camerons, Menzies, and Drummonds. It would be quite the celebration. He heard his wife's voice, so eavesdropped for a few moments.

"Nay, 'tis my color. Ye'll not be changing now, Ysenda."

He recognized that tone in Eli's voice. Ysenda was not going to win this argument. He hid his smirk the best he could.

"But I like it. Why can we no' wear the same? We're sisters."

"Listen, ye conniving harlot, ye cannae have it. Find yer own color." Eli glanced over her shoulder, noticed him by the sideboard and crossed to him with a piece of fabric in her hand. "Look. What do ye think?"

He leaned down to give her a sultry kiss, but she wasn't having it. She cut it short and said, "I need yer opinion. Will this be a good color for my wedding dress?"

"I'll answer yers as soon as ye answer mine. Were ye cursing yer own sister out?"

She sighed and glared at him, tapping her foot. "Aye. She was trying to steal my color. I know her ways."

"Forgive me if I am wrong about this, but I thought brides wore their clan colors."

"We do, but this is for the under gown. The plaid is the skirt and the fold over our shoulder, but we need an under gown and I wish it to be a pretty color. What do ye think of it?"

Alaric took the swatch from her and studied it. "This is blue. Are ye no' wearing my colors?"

She tipped her head to look at him and snatched the cloth out of his hand. "I'm wearing a Ramsay blue skirt, and this is a lovely color for a Ramsay lass. I am a Ramsay or have ye forgotten? And I'm marrying on Ramsay land."

"To a Grant. A red plaid Grant. And ye *were* a

Ramsay, but now ye are a Grant ever since we handfasted. Or have ye forgotten that?"

He knew she would wheedle her way to what she wanted, but he also knew that somehow, when she came down the lane on horseback, there had better be some red plaid showing somewhere. He knew her mind was scheming for some way to win him over. But then he saw something different cross her mind.

Desire.

She did that odd thing with her tongue, darting it out and then back in again. "Dinnae ye think ye should wear yer tunic inside the hall?" Her gaze ran down his bare chest to his belly and below. "Though I must admit, I am thirsty. I could lick that sweat off yer chest."

He chuckled and stared at her, his desire rising just as hers had. He glanced down at the place where her gaze had locked. He'd planned this, and it was working exactly as he wished.

She licked her lips, narrowed her gaze and said, "Follow me." Whirling around, she never looked back because she knew she wouldn't need to, instead swinging those saucy hips of hers in a way that drew his gaze. He smiled with satisfaction. Damn, but this lass of his was sweet.

"And Reyna," she called as she crossed the hall, "if ye wish to find out if I know how lads make lasses happy, put yer ear to the door in a few moments and ye'll learn."

The entire table of cousins erupted into a chorus of hoots and giggles.

But just as Eli's hand landed on the door handle,

the front door opened, and with one look over his shoulder at who it was, Alaric stopped. "Eli, wait."

They both turned around to regard Kyler at the door, a look on his face that Alaric didn't like. Once he spotted Alaric, he strode right over to him.

"There are several Scots outside the gates, and they are asking for yer wife and Wenna. They are no' from any clan we know."

Eli looked furious, but Alaric had already figured it out. "Would one of these Scots be called Egan?"

"Aye. He said he wished to propose to Eli. I told him ye were already handfasted and getting married soon, and he said that she would be marrying him. We tried to send him away, but he refused. My sire went to find Torrian, but I thought ye should be aware."

"Ye would be correct, Kyler, and I thank ye verra kindly." His erection had died as soon as Kyler had told him who was outside. Desire turned to a fury that wouldn't be sated this time until the bastard's heart was on the end of his sword. Eli moved up next to Alaric and he reached for her hand, then kissed her forehead. "I'll go get rid of him, love. He'll no' be bothering ye."

"I'm coming along."

"Eli," he said, holding her by the arms. "If ye are there, ye'll be fueling his demands. I think 'twould be best if ye waited here." He wished she would take his advice but he knew it wasn't her way.

"I'm coming," she said, pulling out of his grip and crossing her arms.

He sighed. She'd follow as soon as he walked out the door. "Fine, but ye'll stay behind me. Promise me that ye'll not step in front of me."

She dropped her arms to her side and leaned forward. "He willnae hurt me. He wishes to marry me."

Her movements told him she was upset, but he also knew she did not understand exactly what was at stake.

"Nay, men like Egan will hurt ye if he wishes to, though he'll likely no' kill ye. But know that he's a bride-stealer. Have ye never heard of the like? He is large enough to overpower you. He'll grab ye and toss ye across his horse in a flash." Alaric crossed his arms to let her know he would not allow anything other than his conditions. She was stubborn, but she had a quick mind.

"A bride-stealer? They exist? Truly?" She glanced at Alaric and then to Kyler, obviously shocked by this term.

Kyler nodded. "Aye, my lady. Some men think stealing a bride is the proper way to get a woman. Not here, but other clans do it often."

Alaric made one more offer. "Eli, do ye agree to stand behind me or beside me?"

She settled a hand on her hip and let out a loud whoosh between pursed lips.

"I can tie ye up if ye dinnae agree."

"Ye'll no' tie me up unless we are in our bedchamber alone." Her gaze narrowed but his widened.

That comment surprised him, but he'd not bend. Eli was his. He'd never love another, and he would no' lose her to the bastard outside.

She finally grumbled a bit but then nodded. "Fine. I agree."

Hell, but he loved her. Feisty, smart, more than a wee bit stubborn. She had fire. If he was going to consider taking the lairdship, he needed a wife who was smart and fiery. Two thoughts crossed his mind.

They made a great pair.

He'd never give her up.

He nodded. "I'll meet him, Kyler. Lead the way." He took Eli's hand and the two followed Kyler out, a few cousins hurrying to follow the trio without saying a word. "I need to stop at the stables to retrieve my weapon."

He strode quickly enough that Eli had trouble keeping up, but she did. Once at the stable, he retrieved his sword, cleaned it, then kissed the blade. Before he sheathed it, Eli's hand stayed his. She leaned over and kissed the blade too, then kissed him.

He thought he saw a bit of misting in her gaze so he leaned down and whispered in her ear. "Elisant Ramsay, I'd never let another touch ye. I love ye."

"'Tis Elisant Grant to ye."

He grinned at that, then took Eli's hand again as they exited the stable. Torrian and Kyle both approached but remained off to the side. He was pleased the chieftain and his second were there to witness what was to take place.

"What the hell do ye want, Egan? She's no' available. Ye still have the broken nose to remind ye. And what rock did ye crawl out from under? Go back to yer kind. Ye'll never patrol with Maitland Menzie either."

Alaric noticed Logan on horseback off in the distance, Gwyneth in front of him. He hoped he knew enough to stay the hell out of this. His keen eyes would miss nothing though, of that he was certain.

Gavin Ramsay came up behind him. "Do what ye must, Grant. If ye need my assistance, ask for it."

Egan looked quite smug, a group of five men behind him, all carrying swords. "We'll fight six of yer men. Winners take their pick of yer archer lasses."

"Ye hedge-born sot," Eli yelled. "Did ye consider asking me first, ye ugly troll?"

"Shut her up!" Egan shouted, pointing his sword at her. It was smaller than any of the Ramsays and Alaric's, a toy in comparison. "Lasses dinnae speak unless they are given permission."

"I'll speak when I wish, ye arsehole." She took a step forward, but stopped as Alaric moved in front of her, his hand crossing the front of her waist to protect her as he moved her behind him. She stuck her head around him and shouted, "And dinnae ever tell me what to do. Ye are as daft as a horsefly."

Eli wanted the last word. He didn't like the way this was going. He'd never guessed the fool wanted six brides. Nor was he expecting six men wishing to fight. He stole a quick glance to assess their weapons. Most were paltry compared to the great swords of the Grants and Ramsays.

Egan's face turned the darkest shade of red he'd ever seen, nearly purple. "I said shut her up." Then he moved so he could look straight at Eli. "When ye are mine, I'll teach ye to listen to me. Ye willnae like it, but ye'll do as ye are told. I'll beat yer arse until ye can do naught but wait on me."

"The hell I will, ye churlish bastard."

Egan made a move toward Eli, but Alaric was faster, unsheathing his sword and stepping farther in front of her, his sword aimed right at Egan's belly. He stared straight into the fool's smug gaze. "Get back. Ye dinnae deserve to stand near her. The battle is between ye and me."

Torrian called out, "I have many guards who will escort them off our land. Yer choice, Grant."

A crowd had begun to gather in a half circle in front of the gates, guards moving wherever Torrian directed them, along with a line of archers on the parapets, but he would not be distracted from his purpose. This would end here and now. He'd had enough of this arrogant bastard's bullshit.

How dare he threaten his wife!

"Nay, Chief, no one speaks to my wife in such a way. I'll take care of him," Alaric replied. "'Twill be my pleasure. This fool wouldn't listen on Cameron land. Now he will. Once ye are dead, Egan, yer friends will take their leave and never come back."

One of the men behind Egan dared to draw

an arrow, aiming it at him, or perhaps Eli behind him. An arrow landed between the fool's feet so fast that the idiot dropped his weapon in shock.

Out of the corner of his eye, Alaric saw Eli's mother with her bow in hand.

"Stand down!" she bellowed. Merewen was as good as her daughter at archery.

Torrian raised his hands. "Stand back, all of ye. This is between Alaric and Egan. Ramsays, unless ye are a guard, ye belong up on the curtain wall."

"Chief?" Gavin asked. "I'd like a good view since this involves my daughter."

"Gavin, ye may stay with yer daughter, but we need room," Torrian said with a wide grin, pointing to a line of approaching horses. Torrian met the group and directed the riders to fan out into a circle surrounding Egan and his men.

Alaric couldn't believe his eyes. First came Grant warriors, including his brothers and his sire. Aye, he was certain he saw Els with Joya on one horse and his father in a cart behind Jowell. Loki Grant's small group was behind them. Then came Menzie warriors, Camerons, and a line of Matheson warriors. The last group was led by Micheil Ramsay, a long line of Drummond warriors now behind Egan's men.

He glanced at Eli who was now grinning from ear to ear. She moved over next to him and stood on her tiptoes, kissing his cheek. "Take care of this, husband. I'll be up on the wall with my weapon and my mama. Ye know what ye need to do."

"I do, lass."

Alaric moved to the middle of the circle, waiting for Egan. As soon as Egan had taken his place, Alaric looked to Torrian.

"Ye give the word, Chief."

Chants and yells of support echoed across the landscape, but he vowed to ignore them, because now he had to focus on one thing and one thing only.

The enemy. His beloved grandfather, the renowned swordsman Alexander Grant, had taught his grandsons how to fight one-on-one with a fool. There'd been much more to it, but his advice came down to one word.

Focus.

"Chief?" Alaric would bow to whatever Torrian wished.

He glanced at the Ramsay chieftain, and Egan showed his true colors.

Out of the corner of his eye, Alaric caught Egan running to his side and attempting to hit him from behind. Alaric's blade swung to defend himself, and their weapons clashed.

The fight was on.

Chapter Thirty-One

E LI GASPED BUT kept quiet. She wouldn't risk distracting her husband.

Alaric planted his feet and said, "Ye cheating piece of slime."

"Take care of him, Grant!" Torrian shouted.

Alaric growled and raised his sword over his head, coming down on Egan's own raised weapon. The clash rang out, followed by another four rapid clashes of the blades. They attacked and parried back and forth, grunting and repositioning themselves, the crowd cheering him on with each blow. Alaric swung his sword in powerful arcs that would surely destroy anything in its path.

Eli watched her husband move as if his sword were a part of him, every move a rhythmic masterpiece. In such a battle to the death, he would surely prevail. His intensity on his target was impressive to watch.

Fighting, taunting, parrying, thrusting. Her husband was magnificent, the muscles on his back rippling with every powerful move.

He battled with a grace and a force that was

unparalleled, but Eli could tell he was playing with the man—teasing him to swing more and more. Egan began to swing wildly, losing his strength and probably sensing it. He changed tactics and reverted to his mouth instead.

"Give her to me. Ye have plenty of lasses." He stopped to pant, glancing up at Eli on the curtain wall. "Or give me another one. I'll let ye have that wise-mouthed bitch and trade her for a sweet one."

"Ye think to insult my wife? Yer comments are a compliment, rather. Ye'll never have her." Alaric taunted. "She is mine."

Eli could kiss him for that comment. Her mother noticed because she squeezed Eli's hand and smiled.

Alaric twirled in a quarter-circle to take him off-guard, then reversed his direction, a move that allowed his blade to catch Egan's leg. First blood.

The crowd roared, but Alaric kept his eyes on his foe. Eli's heart swelled with love for him, and a prayer that he would come through the fight unscathed.

Egan had the nerve to look up at her. "I've a change of mind. I'll keep her. Ye'll be mine soon, lass." Then he formed his lips into a kiss.

Eli almost nocked an arrow, she was so disgusted.

Her husband didn't approve of his move, either, if she were to guess, because his stance shifted into one of even more intense focus. He was done with the taunts and the teases. He was ready to kill.

Alaric swung from the right, then from the left,

knocking the man's weapon out of his hands. Egan scrambled to grab it before Alaric could drive his blade into his chest. Wiping the dirt from his hands, he gripped his small sword and snarled at Alaric.

"We just need three archers to train ours. Just let us have them. And in turn, she'll give me bairns with that skill bred into them already. She'll give me all lads, five of them. We'll come back and take over this castle, driving ye out."

Alaric laughed at the man's foolishness.

"I tire of this, Egan. Say yer goodbyes to yer friends. Tell them to leave and take yer body with them."

"Nay, we'll be taking six lasses with us. And I'll take yer lass and make her mine right in front of ye. I thought ye'd like to watch her scream when I bury myself inside her, ripping her apart."

Eli covered her ears, knowing that was the talk that would make Alaric finally end this fight. She knew he played with Egan, taunting and teasing him into thinking he had a chance when everyone there knew he didn't. It was part of the show, if she had to guess. He had an audience unlike any other—Grants, Ramsay, Menzies, Drummonds, Camerons, Mathesons.

Before Alaric could deliver the killing blow, all five of Egan's friends raised their weapons and charged.

Within seconds, Gavin, Gregor, Broc, Alasdair, Alick, Paden, and a few others got into the battle, stopping it before it even started. The fools saw the size of the swords and the number fighting them, and they froze in their tracks. One man mounted his horse and left.

Alaric made his final assault. One thrust from the left, one from the right, then he twirled in a circle, giving the weapon the power he wanted. At the last moment, he changed his mind and turned the hilt enough that he hit Egan's weapon with the flat of his blade, sending the smaller sword flying too far for the fool to grab it.

It nearly struck one of Egan's own men.

Alaric held his blade to Egan's throat. "Apologize to my wife."

Eli couldn't help herself. "Husband? No apology needed, but I would like my turn!"

Alaric gave her a nearly imperceptible nod, then stepped to the side a bit, giving her a clear shot. She fired her arrow and hit the foul bastard right where she'd aimed.

Right in his bollocks.

Egan screamed like a banshee as he fell to his knees, clutching the arrow and trying to remove it.

Alaric called out, "Nice shot, wife."

"Ye wish to tell me what to do now, Egan?" Eli called.

Egan fainted. The four men who remained mounted their horses and took off without him.

The crowd cheered and applauded.

Out of the corner of her eye, she noticed her grandsire and grandmother heading away from the castle.

She knew what they were doing. She shouted to Alaric who was now in the middle of a crowd, all patting his back and cheering for him. "I'll be right back!"

Racing down the stairs, she grabbed Kyle's horse and mounted with a leap, saying, "I'm just borrowing him for a moment, Kyle." She had to speak to her grandfather.

Catching up to him, she shouted, "Stop! Where are ye going?"

Her grandmother reached for her grandsire's forearm and squeezed it, causing him to slow his horse. "What do ye want, Eli?"

"Nice shot, Granddaughter," her grandmama said with a wink. "Ye make this old woman proud."

Her grandsire shifted in his saddle. "Ye chose a fine man, lass. He handles his sword well. Reminds me of Alex."

"Many thanks, but where are ye taking Grandmama?" She worried they were leaving, never to return. She had to stop them.

"Just for a ride, lass. We'll be back for the wedding."

Somehow, by the look in both sets of eyes, eyes she'd seen nearly every day of her life, she knew he was lying. "Ye are taking her away to die."

"Lass," Grandmama said. "I'll no' die in front of everyone. I'd just like to go peacefully, in the arms of my love."

"Ye cannae go yet. We're all getting married. Ye have to stay for the wedding."

Her grandmother looked at her grandfather. "Fine. Logan, after we go for a ride, we'll come back so we can see the wedding. Then we'll go on our journey."

Her grandfather smiled, set his horse into a gallop and called over his shoulder, "We'll be back for the wedding!"

She knew they weren't coming back. Her grandmother had always said she wished to die privately. He was taking her to her deathbed.

"I know ye are lying!" The tears erupted as she watched the two take one of the side paths off of Ramsay land. "I love ye both!"

Her grandfather waved a hand up in the air, but never turned around.

She set her mount to a trot behind them, tears blurring her view. "Come back," she whispered.

She never saw the horse coming. Suddenly an arm wrapped around her and yanked her off her horse, hauling her over to lie belly down across the saddle of a racing mount.

It was one of Egan's men. "Egan didn't get ye, so I'll take ye instead."

He joined the other four men who waited for him, and they took off down a different path through the forest.

"Instead of five men and five women, it'll be just one of ye. But I think ye are feisty enough to handle all of us."

The bastard had his hand on her arse. "Get yer hands off of me!" She screamed at him but couldn't sit up or wriggle free of the hand holding her down.

"Why? 'Tis a fine arse. I cannae wait to see it with those trews off, and ye'll never wear them again. My wife will wear a skirt at all times, so I can slide my hand up her leg to her bum whenever I wish."

That did it for Eli. What kind of fool did he think she was? She squirmed and fought and finally did what she had to. She punched him between his legs.

He let out a howl and nearly fell off the horse. His hold loosened, and she righted herself so she could jump off.

Except they raced along a ravine she didn't care to jump into. She had to hold on until they were in an area where she could land without killing herself.

She knew Alaric would miss her and would follow soon enough, she just had to be patient.

Patience wasn't something she did very well.

Fortunately, she could hear hoofbeats approaching from behind. She looked behind them and was pleased to see her husband.

"Eli, dinnae jump yet! 'Tis too dangerous. I'll get ye."

Alaric followed Eli's captor along the edge of the ravine, waiting for a safe place to pull up alongside the fool and knock him off his horse. Eli was plenty strong enough to manage the horse and right herself.

If she couldn't, he'd be right there.

But first, he had to calm the fury that raged inside him. He thought of Alexander Grant's words: *An angry, emotional man never wins. Ye have to control yer emotions.*

He hadn't understood how difficult that would be. His fury threatened to overpower his thinking, so he looked at his wife instead of her captor, thinking again how much he adored her. She didn't deserve all this chaos so close to their wedding day.

The ravine gradually shallowed as they rode into an area of the forest that was thick with trees and where the path became wide enough for him to ride abreast of the fool. "Get ready to grab the reins, Eli," he bellowed once he was close enough for her to hear him.

He saw an area up ahead that looked safe enough to make his move. The need to make sure she wasn't hurt was paramount. After Els and his father, he couldn't bear anything happening to his wife.

They reached the wide, flat stretch of the path.

"Grab the reins, Eli! And hold on!"

Alaric kicked his feet free of his stirrups and launched himself across the gap between the two horses. He plowed into other man, knocking him off his horse to the side of the path. They landed with a thump, Alaric landing on top of him hard enough to knock the wind out of the kidnapper. One punch was all it took to knock the swine out cold.

He stood just as his brother Jowell passed him, glancing back at him.

"Stay with her, Jowell! I lost my horse."

He got up and raced down the path, watching

as Eli fought to gain control of the horse. She had the reins, but the frightened horse had bolted and would not heed her.

"Slow him down, Eli!"

Jowell had nearly caught up to her. He would make it!

The horse had to jump over a fallen log and tossed Eli into the air. She landed in a heap.

Alaric thought he would vomit. But he fought through it and found an extra burst of speed.

"Eli! Jowell! Get to her! Eli!" She had to be hale.

Calm down. She'll stand up in a moment and curse at everyone. She'll be fine.

By the time he reached her, Jowell had caught the horse, pulling the panicked beast to the side of the path so it wouldn't step on her. Uncle Connor and Broc came up behind him, but he couldn't talk with them.

Eli lay unmoving in the dirt off to the side of the path. He knelt next to her and kissed her lips first. He didn't know what else to do. For all he'd done for his father and his brother, he was suddenly helpless, unable to act.

"Eli," he whispered. "Come back to me, love. Say anything."

Uncle Connor leaped off his horse and said, "Get a mount. We need to get her out of here and back to the keep. There were three or four other men, and I fear they might return. Take my horse. Broc will find yers." His brother went after his horse.

Alaric nodded, unable to speak. She looked so

pale and helpless, all he could do was pray she would come back to him.

Broc yelled over his shoulder as he left, "One of ye check her for broken bones, Alaric. Stay calm. Do what Mama taught us."

Connor said, "I'll do it. Mount up." He knelt next to her and checked both arms and legs, then felt the back of her head. "None that I can find, and she has no lumps on her head, Alaric, so dinnae go to that place in yer mind. She's young and strong. This ground is softer than when yer sire and brother fell."

He mounted the warhorse and turned it around, then his uncle picked her up carefully, handing her to him.

What else could go wrong?

CHAPTER THIRTY-TWO

ALARIC PACED OUTSIDE the healing chamber. His father sat in a chair not far away, his leg propped, his brother next to him.

"It's not the same, Alaric. She landed on softer ground and not on her head like Els did. I saw her land. She'll come around." Jowell did his best to convince him, but he couldn't hide the worry etched on his face.

Alaric paced and paced.

Torrian handed him a cup of ale. "This is the best place to be. Ye have all the best healers tending her. Brenna, Aunt Jennie, Brigid, Jennet, Tara, and yer mother are all here. The best of the best ye have in there. Have faith in them."

"Verra true. I must apologize for all the trouble we brought to ye, Chief. We had no idea he would follow us here." Alaric took a mouthful of his drink. He hadn't realized how thirsty he was. He'd had nothing since before his training bouts.

"I knew he was naught but trouble, Alaric," Brin said. "Eli will come around. She had no wounds, no visible bump. Mayhap not right away.

Some like to sleep for a while. Helps them heal, my mother always says."

Ceit sat not far away twisting her gown in her lap, and Brin moved over to massage her shoulders.

The door opened and Gracie came out, a smile on her face. That alone settled Alaric a bit. She came straight to him and clasped his shoulder. "She is awake and talking. She was wiggling her toes. These are all good signs. Now I've come to sit with ye while the experts check her over from head to toe. I think she'll be fine, Alaric."

He let out a breath and said, "Thank the Lord above. May I see her, Mama?"

"Wait until Aunt Jennie and Jennet take a good look. Aunt Brenna says they are the best because her eyes are no' what they used to be. Come sit with me."

He nodded. "Ye are right. Did she know where she was? Did she recognize ye all?" He remembered that from somewhere. Someone who woke up and had no idea where they were. All the conversations they'd had about his brother had stuck in his mind.

"She did. Asked if ye were hale, so her mind is working well. Give them another hour with her, and then I'm sure ye can see her. Why do ye no' go clean up and find a tunic? Ye look like ye rolled in the mud." His mother kissed his cheek. "Ye fought well, son."

He glanced down at his chest and belly, just noticing he was covered with dirt. "I guess I could use a quick clean up. I'll jump in the loch later."

Heather came down the stairs, and Torrian called out to her. She motioned to Alaric and led him up the stairs to a chamber, sent a maid to retrieve a basin of fresh water, and asked, "Do ye have a clean tunic? If no', I can find one for ye."

"Nay, I have one in our chamber, Heather. Many thanks to ye. The water would be appreciated."

Heather patted his shoulder and said, "She's in wonderful hands, but ye know that."

"Aye. I'll be just a few moments. In case Eli calls for me."

She nodded and left, closing the door behind her. He flopped onto a stool and let his head fall into his hands, so grateful that Eli would be fine. Once he was able to slow the fast beating of his heart, he cleaned up what he could, then donned the fresh tunic. He didn't have a clean plaid, but he'd get one later.

When he made his way down the stairs, the mood of the group below had changed from fear and sadness to one of joy. Aunt Jennie and Aunt Brenna stood just outside the door of the healing chamber.

Heather raised her arms for everyone's attention "Come, we have much to celebrate. Join us around the hearth, and we'll have the lasses serve the evening meal. So many have arrived, and we are ready for ye! Plenty of food and drink for all."

The group moved away, their happiness glowing on their faces. Alaric spotted many good friends and family who he couldn't wait to greet, but Eli came first. As he watched the group, he was pleased to see Jowell had already seated his father in a chair near the hearth, propping his leg.

Gavin came over to him. "Many thanks for what ye did. 'Tis an honor to have ye as a part of our clan and as a son-in-law. I know ye will take good care of my lassie. Ye fight like Alex did. In fact, if not for the fair hair, ye look much like yer grandsire."

"Many thanks to ye, Gavin. May I see her? Have ye seen her?"

"I told Merewen ye get first rights to our lassie, and she agreed. She's speaking with Aunt Brenna. Go on in. Take yer time. We'll enjoy our guests."

He stepped past so many people that they all began to meld together in his mind. So many claps on his back and words of congratulation, but his mind was only on the lass behind the door.

He'd had such a fear when he glanced back over at her grandparents leaving and saw Eli on a horse alone and suddenly grabbed by one of Egan's friends. He left Egan to the Ramsays and grabbed the nearest horse to go after her.

The bastard had taken a treacherous path. He knew any jump or fall as they raced along the ravine could have been dangerous for either of them. But they were both here safe.

Aunt Jennie approached him when he neared the door. "She's fine, Alaric. I know Eli to be a tough lass, but she's pretty shaken up by the entire situation. She sports a few bruises on her body so do be gentle with her, but she'll have no lasting issues from her fall. Ye did a fine job saving her from that fool.

"I swear that my mother was the wisest woman on earth for telling all of us that we had to allow our bairns to choose their own partners. Yet some fools persist in this ridiculous bride-stealing practice." Then she leaned in to whisper, "I dinnae think Eli believed they would dare try to steal her away, but 'tis now in her past. Fear no'. She'll be up and walking in no time. She's asking for ye. Jennet is helping her to change out of her torn clothing into a clean gown just now."

"Many thanks to ye, Aunt Jennie."

She patted his cheek and said, "Ye look just like my brother except for that light hair on yer head and those blue eyes. Yer mother passed her beauty on to ye."

He blushed a bit at that comment, but the door opened and Jennet and Brigid both came out, Jennet coming right over to him. "She's asking for ye. I told her to rest for a wee bit. She is exhausted and a bit bruised. But the bride stealing attempt has thrown her off kilter."

"Do me a favor, Jennet," Alaric said. "Keep the others out for a wee bit? I'd like to be alone with her."

Jennet patted his forearm. "I'll send Ethan over as guard. No one will dare question him."

"Many thanks." Then he moved over to the door, took a deep breath to steel himself for any bruises or scrapes on his dear wife, then opened the door.

The room was dim, and Eli lay on the bed in the back of the chamber. "Eli, ye are hale? Please tell me so, love."

"Alaric? I'm so glad ye are here." She held out her hand to him, a silent request for him to come closer.

He stepped over to her side, pleased when she moved over in the bed and patted the spot next to her. That was all he needed to see. He dropped his dirty plaid and slid in next to her, wrapping his arms around her and holding her close to breathe in her essence just for a moment.

"I was so scared when ye flew off that horse, lass."

"I was so scared when that bastard kidnapped me. He wanted me to take on all five of them, and he told me I'd never wear leggings again, and..."

"Hush, I'm here now. Ye know I will always protect ye, do ye no'?" He leaned back and lifted her chin up to look at him, dropping a quick kiss on her lips.

She nodded, her eyes damp. "I do. I nearly jumped off into the ravine, but I told myself I had to wait until ye followed. I knew ye would. I love ye."

"I love ye too. And I love that ye are a strong lass, wife of mine. I counted on ye being strong, and ye were."

"Make love to me, Alaric."

"Och, naught would please me more, but I can see a bruise on yer cheek and a cut under yer chin. Jennet said ye are bruised elsewhere from the fall. I fear I might hurt ye because my need for ye is so bad. We should probably wait."

"Nay. Now, Alaric."

"I know ye wanted me before we were rudely interrupted, as I did ye, but much has changed."

"Aye, that was a desire. This is a need for ye, husband. A need that I have to know that we are still us. That those fools didn't change what we have."

"Promise me that ye will stop me if I hurt ye?"

"Ye cannae hurt me."

Alaric slid his hand under her gown to feel her soft skin, moving his hand down to part her curls, teasing her to prompt her juices to flow. He kissed her neck, played with her breasts until she moaned a bit too loudly, then pressed on. When she spread her legs, she was already slick with her need for him.

"We will do this slowly, lass."

"Aye. Please. I need ye inside me, Alaric. Ye and me together forever."

He did his best to settle her on her side so he could slip inside her, pleased to find that it was easier than he'd expected.

"Ye did need me, lass of mine." He slid in as deep as he could, his hand going to her bottom to pull her against him so he could fill her.

She moaned and he set his lips on hers to catch the sound. Ethan was out there, and he knew how loud his wee wife could be when their lovemaking turned wild. He vowed that this would not be wild, but slow.

He moved inside her, gauging her need, thrusting in and out until she caught his rhythm and they danced together, slipping in and out in a slow beat unlike their usual, a feeling so powerful that he feared he'd go before her.

"Ye arenae hurting anywhere?"

"Hell, nay, ye brawny brute."

He grinned. "Yer wish is my command, my queen. Tell me what ye want."

"Faster. I need ye faster and harder."

He did what he could under the circumstances, but he decided to reach down and help her peak faster, finding the spot that would propel her over the edge.

As soon as he found it, she moaned again and spread her legs wider and he moved her onto her back because he could no longer restrain himself.

When he was finally settled above her, his weight on his elbows to protect her, he whispered, "Look at me, Elisant."

She opened her eyes and gazed up at him, a look of sheer desire on her face. Her hand cupped his cheek, and she said, "Finish this now."

"I'll always protect ye, Eli. I will always be there for ye."

"And I for ye."

His lips melded against hers, and he pounded into her, needing to finish quickly. As soon as he heard her go over the edge, her contractions seizing him, he followed, holding his yell inside as best he could as he finished.

Gazing into her eyes, he saw the same sense of awe he felt.

"Och, but ye are a fine bull, husband. Slow was better than fast mayhap."

He chuckled and rolled off her, tugging her with him. "I'm so grateful ye are hale."

She leaned up on her elbow so she could look at him. "I worried about ye a wee bit in the sword fight, but as soon as I saw ye trade blows, I knew he didnae stand a chance against my big, strapping man. Yer weapon is such a delight."

He had to laugh at this, glancing over at her with a smirk then kissing her fingertips.

"Alaric, do ye wish I would stop cursing? I could, if ye truly want me too. It might take a while though."

He grinned and said, "Nay, I love ye just the way ye are, Queenie. I dinnae think I've ever been so proud as when ye told the bastard to shut his mouth. I nearly dropped my sword to kiss ye, but I couldnae."

"I love ye just the way ye are too. Now get yer arse out of this bed. I need some food."

He climbed out of bed and helped her out, finding a basin and ewer of fresh water on the table. He washed and helped her to wash up, then donned his plaid and dressed her in a night rail over the gown Jennet had provided.

When he opened the door, there stood Ethan, his arms crossed in front, guarding the door.

A dozen of their cousins stood facing him: Braden, Roddy, Rose, Daniel, Constance, Wulf, Reyna, Broc, Paden, Cadyn, and behind them all, John and Coira.

Alaric and Eli froze for a moment, surprised by

the gathering, then they broke into laughter and stepped out. When Alaric regained his composure, he held up his hand.

"She's fine now."

Daniel stepped forward to greet them. "We heard. We're happy for both of ye."

Ethan took a step toward Daniel, and Alaric grasped his shoulder. "Thanks, Ethan. Ye can go back with Jennet. Ye did a fine job."

"My honor, Alaric. I hope ye enjoyed yer reunion."

"We did," he replied.

Ten voices called out, "We know!"

"Well, if ye thought my wife would blush, I'll tell ye she'll no'."

Eli grinned, and Alaric couldn't resist—he gave her a smacking kiss for all to see.

CHAPTER THIRTY-THREE

THE WEDDING WAS going to be glorious. More than that—it would be stunning, beautiful, wonderful. So many things to Eli. The days had passed as they'd readied the keep for the festivities, and it would be nearly perfect.

Except her grandparents weren't there.

"Eli, I need ye to promise me something," her mother said.

"I'll try. But I know they are no' coming back. And it's my wedding—and everyone else's nearly."

"Ye are already handfasted and so are the others," Merewen said. "Promise me ye will no' allow their absence to ruin yer day. Ye deserve every happy moment, and so does Alaric. And the others. No tears."

"I'll try, Mama. But I hoped she would come back, with Brigid and Jennet and Tara all here."

"She visited with them and said her goodbyes. None of them had any new treatments for her to try, but Brigid gave her something to ease her pain."

Her father came into her bedchamber.

"Merewen, go downstairs and break yer fast. I'll talk with her."

Eli's mother kissed her cheek and slipped out of the chamber.

"Did they tell ye they werenae coming back, Da? Because I could tell they didnae mean to." She fought to hold her tears back. Dammit, but all those years she spent not crying must have built too many up inside her.

"Da called us in to sit with Mama. He came back late one night and called all my siblings to meet with them. It was Molly, Maggie, Simone, Beatris, Sorcha, Gregor, and Brigid. She told us she wouldnae die in front of a crowd. That if she was going to pass on, she wished to do it quietly and without the whole family hovering outside her door. She asked Da to take her away."

"They could have waited a few more days."

"Mayhap, but she has the right to die on her own terms."

"Da, I dinnae wish to live without Grandmama. Grandsire will come back, will he no'?"

"I'm sure he will. Brigid wondered if he was secretly taking her to some other healer. She also said that some people heal on their own, so that is possible too."

Eli hugged her father, so glad to have him by her side. He was her rock through everything. "I know they cannae live forever. I just wished for a wee bit more time."

"But today is yer wedding day, and ye have a fine husband waiting for ye. I have to admit, I didnae think my Elisant would ever find a man who was her perfect match, but Alaric Grant is, I think. Ye have strong feelings for him and he feels the same for ye, so I hope ye will have a wonderful marriage."

"My thanks, Da." She brushed her tears away. "I'll be fine now. I wish for this wedding to begin already!"

"I'll let yer mother know that ye are going to get dressed. I need to prepare, too."

Her father left and her mother returned. Eli readied herself, even going to another chamber so Avelina could do her hair. She knew Lily and her daughters were tacking and decorating the horses, and she couldn't wait to see their mounts. All of a sudden, her nerves tied up in knots from worry about what Alaric would think of her dress.

Much later, all dressed and ready to go, her mother held her by the shoulders at arm's length. "Ye are beautiful, my dear. Yer man will be struck speechless. Ye are ready?"

Eli glanced toward the window of the chamber. "Just one more moment, Mama. Is there nothing more we need to do?"

"Eli, we must go. Ye are late."

"I know. I had hoped…"

Merewen wrapped her arms around her. "Grandmama is no' returning. The others are waiting. 'Tis time."

She squared her shoulders and said, "Ye are correct, Mama. I love ye so. I am ready. I canno' wait to see Alaric in his Grant finery."

Her mother followed her downstairs, but when she saw her father, she stopped, suddenly overcome with emotion because it had been so long since she'd seen him dressed so fine. The white leine against his bronzed skin and the blue of the Ramsay plaid was indeed splendid. And the dark boots he'd had made special were magnificent. Her mother's voice carried over her shoulder, "Oh, Gavin. Ye are as handsome as the day we married."

She hurried over to her sire and kissed his cheek. "Da, ye look wonderful!"

"Ye better get outside. Yer groom is getting nervous, and everyone else is waiting."

"I will. But why would he be nervous?" she asked as she stepped out the door and gazed across the courtyard, full of her cousins and horses. Everyone was just so...

"Eli, ye havenae changed yer mind, have ye?" There stood Alaric, the finest looking man in the entire land. Oh how she adored him.

She shook her head, raced down the stairs and threw herself into his arms. "Never! I love ye, and I'm sorry I delayed."

"As long as ye still agree to say aye, all is forgiven."

"Of course I'll say aye. I wish to be with ye forever, Alaric. Yer heart is entwined with mine. I know no' how it happened, but we'll never be separated."

"True. We may be apart, but I will always love ye, lassie mine." He kissed her cheek then stepped back to look at her gown, walking in a slow circle around her. "Clever, lass."

"Do ye like it?" She rubbed her cheek, hoping he'd say he approved.

"I do," he said, taking in the way she'd managed to mix both plaids. The underskirt of her gown was blue with a Ramsay plaid over it, and her bodice was a light red with a Grant plaid folded over the chest and her shoulder. "Why Grant on top?"

She touched her hand to her chest. "Closest to my heart. But I am both Ramsay and Grant, ye are aware." Her plaid bodice matched his own plaid exactly, his white leine such a contrast against the colors that he looked more magnificent than ever.

"Aye, ye are, my fine beauty. I approve yer choices. Ye will be the loveliest bride there."

Torrian called out, "I'm heading out. Follow me." Torrian and Heather led the way through the gates on horseback and took a small turn toward the loch where the ceremony was to take place.

There were many horses and rows and rows of well-wishers. She and Alaric were last behind Ysenda and Lewis and Tevis and Wenna. Thea and Willum led the group. The parents of each couple escorted them, Gracie and Jamie on one side of them while her parents rode on the other, moving back and forth between Ysenda and Eli. Alaric held her close on their black destrier, ribbons of red and blue entwined in Midnight Moon's mane and tail.

It was a glorious procession. "I love being at the back, Alaric, so we can see everyone. Look how beautiful Ysenda is." Her sister spun around and waved to her. She fought the tears, swiping at them as soon as they appeared. As they made the bend, she thought she caught a flash of something silver at the top of the hill not far away. "Did ye see that, Alaric?"

"Nay, what?"

"A flash of something like a sword. Up in the trees and the brush atop the hill."

"I dinnae see anything, but Kyle and Kyler are patrolling the outskirts with a group of guards, so dinnae worry. No one will try to grab ye on this day. We are surrounded by friends."

"Good," she replied, but she had the oddest feeling that they were being watched. Grandsire and Grandmama? She dismissed it from her mind; she was too busy taking in the sight of the lovely processional. She vowed to enjoy every bit of their wedding day.

Horses pranced and minstrels played as they approached the loch, the parents moving back while the couples moved into a semi-circle around the priest, dismounting and standing together, taking their vows as a group. It almost felt as if they were pledging themselves not only to their spouses, but to their clanmates and friends.

When the ceremony finished, Alaric kissed her hard, then swooped her up and tossed her into the air, catching her as she squealed in delight. She'd never been happier.

They mounted their horse, Alaric climbing behind her as the couples joined their individual clans, banners waving and their horses galloping across the meadow to applause, competing war whoops so loud that at one point, Eli covered her ears. How she loved all their clans.

"Alaric."

"What love?" He let out another Grant war whoop, kissed her cheek and said, "Are ye no' happy?"

"I've never been happier."

Gradually, the shouts and chaos settled, and everyone made their way back to the castle. The courtyard filled with guests and the newly married couples. The families ate and danced in the courtyard, while villagers and guards celebrated outside the wall with food and drink for all.

At one point, Els stood in the center of the dance area, holding his young son and dancing in place. He didn't move his feet, because he was still unsteady, but Joya danced on one side of him while Jowell was on the other to support him. He looked so happy standing and wiggling to the music while his son giggled joyously.

Eli danced until her feet hurt, but she enjoyed every moment of it, especially when Alaric grabbed her and planted a big kiss on her lips while the crowd cheered. They had so much fun, and she made the best of it.

But a wee part of her still missed her grandparents.

When the magical day ended and people began to take their leave, she and Alaric decided to go outside the wall and speak with the villagers and guards and say good eve to those who were leaving. Darkness would be falling soon, and most wished to be settled before night was completely upon them. Rows and rows of colorful tents decorated the meadow for as far as she could see.

She swore she'd never seen so many people in one place. It was a wedding to remember.

It was then, as guests were streaming away, that she saw the reflection up on the hill. Her grandsire's sword. He was there. She swore he was up there watching. That was exactly what she thought she'd seen earlier.

Alaric was busy chatting with some guards, and she laid her hand on his arm to get his attention. "I'll be right back."

He nodded his agreement, and she raced up the hill, oblivious to the dirt on her dress and the rips in her silk hose. She didn't care. She had to see Grandmama one more time.

"Grandmama!" she shouted, hoping it would stop them from taking their leave. "One more time, Grandda, please! Grandmama!"

She reached the top of the hill and pushed through the brush, ignoring the brambles scratching her arm and the nettles against her legs. She didn't care.

She made it into the clearing. The place she was sure they'd been watching from. There! She saw it, her heart nearly exploding from the excitement that they might still be here. The chair. They had been at her wedding.

That knowledge alone pleased her.

There in the middle of the small clearing sat the chair that Donnan and Bethia had made for her grandmother. And across from it was an open area in the brush for them to peer through without giving their location away. Her grandfather was forever clever.

"Grandsire?"

All quiet. Nothing stirred at all. She moved over and brushed her fingers along the back of the chair, tears misting her eyes as she thought about the woman who'd guided her so much in her life.

The woman who'd taught her to be strong, to stand up to men, to stand up for what was right.

The woman who taught them all that a lass could be as powerful in warfare and everyday life as a man.

The woman who loved her children and grandchildren unconditionally, with every part of her being. The woman who taught her the meaning of love.

She would never forget her. She wandered through the small area, hoping she would catch a glimpse of one of them watching from afar, but she didn't.

She was nearly ready to give up when she saw it. Her breath caught as she reached for the medal hanging in the hollow of an ancient tree.

Could it be the medal Grandmama had told her about? She took it from the middle of the tree, fingering the fine chain it was on and studying the delicate pattern of knots engraved on the front before flipping it over to read the words on the back.

The finder of this medal is the chosen one of the faeries. They leave it where they know she will find it.

She clutched the medal in her fist, holding it close to her breast.

She was the chosen one? What exactly did that mean?

Alaric called out through the brush. "Eli? Where are ye?"

"Here. I'm here, love."

He stopped in front of her, looking her up and down. "Ye made a mess of yer dress, aye?"

"I guess. But I dinnae need it anymore."

He gave her that devious look she loved so much.

"What brought ye here, lass?" He reached up and did his best to tame the curls that had come loose from her hairpins in her hurry to reach the top of the hill.

"I thought I saw Grandda and Grandmama here. And look, their chair is behind ye. Proof that they were here."

"Och, so they were. So they did watch us get married. In fact, I see the small area in the bushes that someone cut with a blade. A hole to view everything from without being seen. Sounds like something yer grandsire would do. That pleases ye, does it no'?"

"It does. And I found this necklace in the tree, so I think I'll wear it." She put it on, hiding it under the neckline of her gown.

"In the tree? Did yer grandmother leave it for ye to find?"

She hadn't considered that.

She shrugged. It didn't really matter. No matter

what, the necklace would always remind her of Gwyneth Ramsay.

Eli kissed her husband, then led him back down the hill, taking one last look at the chair.

Then she winked. Just in case someone was there to see.

EPILOGUE

A FTER THE SWORD dance ended, the very last part of the night for those inside the courtyard, Torrian Ramsay came into the center, making his way to the platform.

Alaric and Eli had just returned from the hill. A few people teased her about the condition of her gown, but typical of his feisty wife, Eli didn't rise to the bait. He held her hand with a firm grip, not willing to let go of her. They were now husband and wife forever.

None of this year and a day bullshit.

Eli was his, now and forevermore.

Torrian called all the clan chieftains up to the platform, naming them one at a time.

Connor Grant and Jamie Grant, with wives Sela and Gracie.

Diana Drummond with husband Micheil Ramsay.

Drew Menzie with wife Avelina.

Marcas Matheson with Brigid.

Aedan Cameron with Jennie.

Loki Grant with Arabella.

Once all had gathered with him, Torrian spoke to everyone in the courtyard.

"We have some announcements to make. We all met earlier today, before the wedding, and decided to do this while we are all together. Some are aware, and some will be surprised. We have many changes to announce. First, Aedan and Jennie Cameron."

Aedan and Jennie introduced Brin as the new Cameron laird and sang the praises of his wife, Ceit.

Diana Drummond and Micheil Ramsay announced that the next laird of Clan Drummond would be their son David and celebrated his marriage to Anna.

Marcas Matheson announced that he was remaining as laird of Clan Matheson. He and his wife Brigid were welcoming their son Merek as co-laird.

Loki announced that Kenzie would be the new laird of Castle Curanta.

Drew Menzie and wife Avelina announced that their son Tad was the new laird of Clan Menzie. Ada applauded while a lad on Maitland's shoulders shouted, "Look, Wiley. 'Tis our da!" Quin smiled and pointed to the platform while Wiley held on to Maeve's hand.

Torrian took the dais again with his wife Heather. "'Tis time for a new lairdship at Clan Ramsay, as well. I agree with my sire that the lairdship should be passed on while the laird can still give guidance. Thus, I announce that Clan Ramsay is moving to co-lairdship because we have grown so large. The two lairds will be our son, Lachlan, and Errol, son of Gavin and Merewen.

Connor Grant was next, and with Jamie at his side, said, "We have deliberated much over this decision, but we are happy with our choice. We are passing on the co-lairdship of Clan Grant to Alasdair, son of Jake and Aline, and Alick, son of Kyla and Finlay."

The two joined them, ecstatic with the announcement.

But everyone looked at Alaric and Eli. Everyone had assumed this would go to Alaric.

Alaric whispered to Eli, "Dinnae worry. They will all learn the truth soon."

Torrian congratulated everyone, and as everyone rejoined their clans, he waited for the group to settle before announcing the next speaker.

"Our last speaker is my dearest mother, Brenna Grant Ramsay." Everyone cheered Brenna on as he helped her to manage the high step. He stood behind her as she made her announcement.

Brenna began, her cracking voice telling all how important this announcement was to her, "I have a verra special announcement to make, and this comes from Logan and King Robert, who has been grateful for all the help we gave him while he was away from Scotland assisting his brother. The Battle of Skaithmuir was a decisive victory for the Scots on our land, and Sir James

Douglas considers it one of his most difficult battles ever. He sings the praises of our wonderful young people who were there to help him.

"Because of this, King Robert has awarded Clan Ramsay another castle, one that you will learn more about soon enough. But we are here to announce who we, as a group, have unanimously chosen to be chieftains of this new property and the clan that will grow there."

She stopped to mop her tears before continuing, and Torrian squeezed her shoulders in support. "This is what Quade always dreamed, to have his bloodline, the Ramsay bloodline in many clans. So now we are part of the Grants and the Drummonds and the Menzies." She paused to mop her tears again. "And the Camerons and Mathesons. And now we will be a part of this new clan."

Brenna stopped, dried her tears one last time, then smiled at everyone. "We'd like to call the following to come forward: Alaric Grant, Elisant Ramsay Grant, Maitland Menzie, and Dyna Grant Corbett."

Alaric squeezed Eli's hand and ushered her in front of him, meeting Maitland and Dyna at the dais.

Once they were there, Brenna turned the four around.

"We are verra fortunate that these four wonderful young people have agreed to start a new clan. They will decide exactly who the two lairds will be, and it is their choice. But we have come up with a new name.

"Welcome the leaders of our new ally, Clan Grantham."

The End

http://www.keiramontclair.com/

DEAR READER,
Yes! You have a whole new clan to look forward to. I haven't worked out all the details, but know that this clan will be some distance away from their allies.

The Battle of Skaithmuir was a real battle fought with Sir James Douglas leading the Scots. This was the battle that earned him the nickname "the Black Douglas." I tried to stay as true to history as I could when it came to the famine and the starving English left in Berwick Castle to fend for themselves. That part is true.

The group of female archers at Skaithmuir took place only in my mind. This part and the rest is fiction.

This new clan, Clan Grantham, will start fresh, bring you new people to love.

Oh, you will occasionally see old friends, but not often. I plan for this to be entirely new. Maybe an island? Maybe on Black Isle? I don't know yet. I haven't decided.

But you will see the following:

Maitland and Maeve

Dyna and Derric

Alaric and Eli.

And you just might see Logan Ramsay again.

I love each of these characters, and from what you tell me, you do too. So I think this will be a wonderful fresh start. Stay tuned in the fall to find out. I have to work it all out in my head over the summer.

Thanks for reading!

Keira Montclair

Novels by Keira Montclair

ABOUT THE AUTHOR

KEIRA MONTCLAIR IS the pen name of an author who lives in South Carolina with her husband. She loves to write fast-paced, emotional romance, especially with children as secondary characters.

When she's not writing, she loves to spend time with her grandchildren. She's worked as a high school math teacher, a registered nurse, and an office manager. She loves ballet, mathematics, puzzles, learning anything new, and creating new characters for her readers to fall in love with.

She writes historical romantic suspense. Her bestselling series is a family saga that follows two medieval Scottish clans through three generations and now numbers over forty books.

Contact her through her website:
www.keiramontclair.com